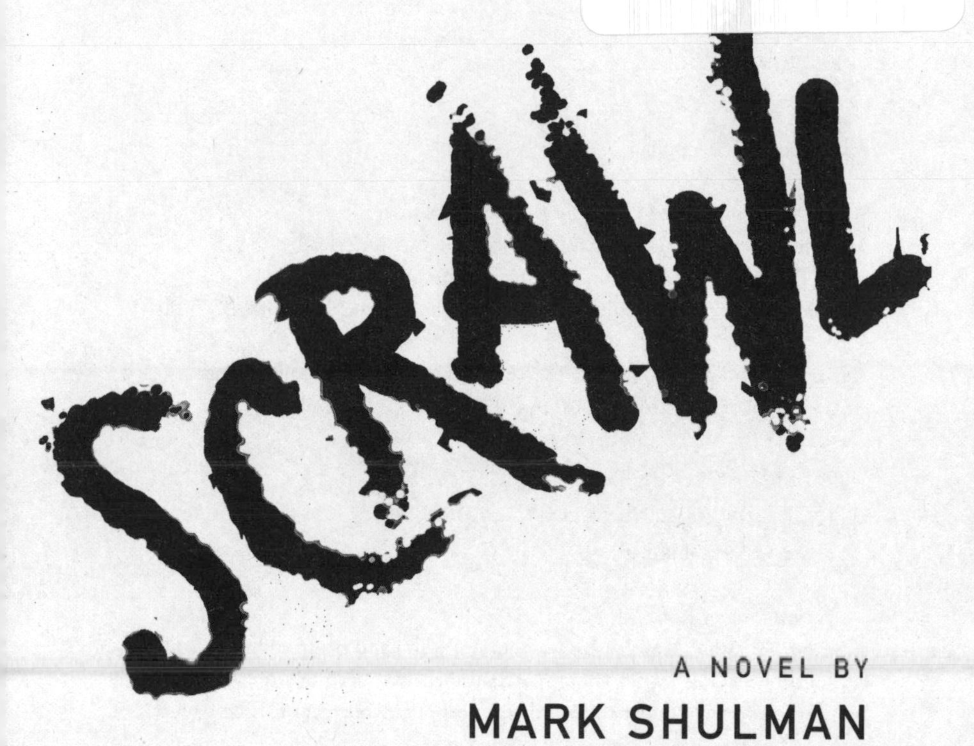

A NOVEL BY

MARK SHULMAN

Roaring Brook Press
New York

For Kara, who reads me

An Imprint of Macmillan

 Printed in the United States of America by
R. R. Donnelley & Sons Company, Harrisonburg, Virginia.
For information, address Square Fish, 175 Fifth Avenue, New York, NY 10010.

Library of Congress Cataloging-in-Publication Data

Shulman, Mark, 1962–
Scrawl / Mark Shulman.
p. cm.
"A Neal Porter Book."
Summary: When eighth-grade school bully Tod and his friends get caught committing a crime on school property, his penalty—staying after school and writing in a journal under the eye of the school guidance counsellor—reveals aspects of himself that he prefers to keep hidden.
ISBN 978-1-250-01269-2
[1. Self-perception—Fiction. 2. Poverty—Fiction. 3. Bullies—Fiction. 4. Schools—Fiction. 5. Diaries—Fiction.] I. Title.
PZ7.S559445Sc 2010
[Fic]—dc22

2010010521

Originally published in the United States by
Neal Porter Books/Roaring Brook Press
First Square Fish Edition: August 2012
Square Fish logo designed by Filomena Tuosto
macteenbooks.com

10 9 8 7

AR: 4.3 / LEXILE: 650L

Wednesday, October 27

Think about a pair of glasses for a second. You see them every day but you really don't think about them, I bet. They're just glass and metal, or glass and plastic. Little pieces of glass stuck on your face that mean everything. Maybe they mean you're smart. Maybe they mean you're rich. But definitely they mean you can't see without them. Grind the glass this way, put in a slight curve, and you can see far. Change that curve a hair, just a tiny, minuscule difference, and you can see near. Grab the two lenses between your big hands and twist your wrist—just *snap* the part over the nose—now you can't see anything for the rest of the day. That's how it went for fat Ricardo Manzana.

The bell rang for English class and I'd promised Mr. Harmon I wouldn't be late again. I got up off Ricardo's chubby back, peeled myself off that authentic, autographed blue hockey sweatshirt he wears every day with the stupid hole in it, and I wiped off my big old carpenter pants. Ricardo was pathetic sprawled on the hall floor, not crying this time but blinking a lot and not talking either, like he was in bed that morning and he didn't want to get up and go to school for some reason.

That's the bell, Ricardo. Time to get up. Kids were starting to walk around us and look, but they steered plenty clear of me. Mostly they looked at Ricardo facedown on the sick green dusty floor next to the overflowing trash can. That's when I noticed the orange peel next to the bright blue can for the first time, close by Ricardo's tangled hair, but I really had to go.

Reaching down and helping Ricardo up would be a good idea. Usually they aren't so quick to narc if you do something nice, something unexpected just before you walk away. I reached down with my hand thoughtfully, and I smiled, and I pulled Ricardo onto his fat stupid feet. I kept that smile going while I fogged up both halves of his glasses with my breath and wiped away my thick thumbprints. Just before I sauntered down the empty hall to class, I pressed the parts straight into his trembly palm. (Mrs. W., is *trembly* a word or should I have used *trembling*?)

They're not even really glass, you know, almost never. Glass is easier to break than plastic. But I think it would be mean to crack the lenses. I guess we'll always call them glasses anyway.

I ran down the

Tuesday, October 19

Call me Tod.

Okay, no, I'm just kidding. That's the first line from *Moby Dick,* all right? I always wanted to start a book like that. This is my first book, and I'm writing it for one reason only. Not for history and not for scientific research and definitely not to let out my inner demons. I'm doing it so I don't have to pick up trash in the school courtyard like certain deviant so-called friends of mine who also got caught.

I am being reformed.

The story begins with me, your humble narrator, alone and stranded after school in a Study Hall the exact same color as puke. I'm a prisoner caught in the fluorescent searchlights, looking pale green while I smudge blue ink in a black-and-white marble composition book. The floor is the same sad green as my pants, but my pants are a lot cleaner. My white pad of paper looks a little green, too.

When I looked up and asked you, "What do you want me to write about?" you said, "About anything."

About anything? Okay. Fine with me. You asked for it. I'll write about this desk.

I hate this desk. It's nothing but a slab of plastic connected to my chair by a flimsy metal rod. Did you know that if you're strong enough, you can twist the desk part up and around until it looks like an arm shrugging? Somebody has been doing that all over school. You know, if you put a lefty desk and a righty desk next to each other the right way, the desks really seem like they're saying "I don't care." They look about as bored and uninterested as the rest of us.

[Tod, do you really believe your feelings apply to every student?]

[So you're going to write in my notebook?]

[When I feel the need.]

There's a small cage under the chair that's not big enough to hold half of the huge textbooks they make us carry. How come we have to carry a year's worth of math when we're only working on three pages a week? Can't they come up with smaller textbooks they could give us every month so We The People Who Do The Homework don't have to lug eleven trees back and forth every day? Especially the kids who'd rather sell their monthly welfare bus pass than use it.

This is taking so long to write. I can hear the huge prison clock buzzing and clicking every sixty seconds when the minute hand shifts. I'm actually grateful that they wasted money last year on these cheap loud clocks instead of better ones or air-conditioning.

Each minute, another *tick!* interrupts the teacher and comforts me—I'm one tick closer to the end of the class, the end of the day, the end of school forever. The clocks have huge numbers so the blind kids can read them. I'm not kidding, either. They probably *tick!* so the blind kids can share the equal opportunity of knowing how long the class is going to drag out, like the way elevators beep for every floor they pass. I think it's weird we have those blind inclusion kids. Isn't there a special school they can go to?

What else is in the room? There's a cracked brown flowerpot with a dead stick in it. The stick was probably a plant. It's got a red ribbon hanging off it like you would find on the corner of a diploma or if you won the Spelling Bee. The ribbon says "Congratulations," but who the hell knows why? Congratulations, you finally got a low-paying teaching job. Congratulations, you just got tenure in a school full of mouth-breathers who can't spell "TV." Congratulations, you retired and didn't die of boredom teaching the same idiocy to idiots who care less about what's in your mind than what's in your car. Congratulations, you just put your new plant on a baking-hot radiator in a room that overlooks a brick wall in a crappy part of town. Congratulations, we're entrusting you with the mascot of our school. It's a dead stick.

I'm sitting next to a chalkboard powdered with layers of dust. It makes me sick to breathe. The board is framed with some kind of dark wood that was probably pretty nice in its day. You can tell somebody cared then. All over the school I see that kind of wood where it hasn't been painted or fallen down or ripped out. It's smooth and has a nice pattern in it, or whatever real wood pattern is called. Too bad it's chipped and gouged and splintered and covered with graffiti from wannabe crime kingpins leaving their mark on the world. When you're an adult, you express yourself with flowers, and they die on the radiator. When you're a kid, you make your name with fat-tip markers and carving knives. And you live forever.

Grain. The wood pattern is called a grain.

And there's you. You're reading this, Mrs. W., so I'm sure not going to say anything about the only other person in this miserable field of seven hundred desks. Okay? I wrote enough words. I'm done for today.

Wednesday, October 20

Tod, you did well on your first day in your detention journal. Keep it up and we'll make it smoothly through the month. Please take a look at yesterday's writing. I'll be adding a few notes to what you write, and I'd like you to read them. Feel free to respond to those notes or ask me any questions. But ask me in writing. And I'd like at least the same number of words today. —Mrs. Woodrow

At least the same number of words? You mean you actually want more?

[No, this is an acceptable amount.]

I don't know—my arm might fall off. Then what would I be? A one-armed bandit. Are you *sure* this isn't some kind of jail sentence? It must be one for you, too. I can't believe you got stuck with the job of babysitting me in this rat hole every afternoon. What did *you* get caught doing?

Here we are tied to these desks after school, me with this cruddy notebook and you with your stack of papers and envelopes to go through. Come to think of it, I'm sure all the other kids are jealous that I have my very own guidance counselor. If those long talks in your office didn't sink in . . . and the meetings with my mom didn't shape me up . . . why do you think I'm going to be sitting here every single afternoon, pencil in hand, brain on hold, humming lullabies and staying out of trouble?

[I have my reasons.]

I know what you think. You think I'm fixable, don't you? You want to fix the bad guy. You don't know the half of it. You don't even know why we got caught. Some people will say the streets are safer with me locked away from my fund-raising activities. But are they right? I actually have a calming effect on certain potential troublemakers, and I often stop them from going through with their half-baked plans.

And another thing. Sitting here with you spares me from all kinds of unpleasant interactions with the armed rental cops. You teachers call them "sentries." We call them "the clowns in brown." Being up here in Study Hall means I don't have to deal with those uniformed ex-wrestlers or nasty neckless gym teachers ragging on me for not being the star quarterback or not doing the six-minute mile or not wearing a jockstrap or spitting in the locker room. And up here there are no sudden surprises from the janitors when they show up where they shouldn't. No unfair security cameras either.

Actually, detention makes a handy place to steer clear of the lower class of the lower class after school. Every neighborhood downtown has its own violent Neanderthal troglodyte hell-raisers. One particular un-neighborly neighbor likes to keep me on my toes at home. You might remember him from the eight times he was held back in school. He has a long memory, longer arms, and an IQ like a school-zone speed limit.

> *[Tod, that was a good simile but no more cursing, please.]*

> [Hell isn't a swear word. It's a neighborhood. The Number 8 bus will take you there.]

Here's another good reason to waste away in here. With lifetime penmanship detention, I don't have to come home and give my mom's husband new reasons why I still haven't gotten an after-school job. It wouldn't matter. It's not like they're suddenly going to cut off my supply of macaroni and cheese and instant mashed. Even if by some fluke of nature I ended up bagging groceries, on the first day of work I'd melt the assistant junior manager with my laserbeam opinions. In the amount of time it took to read this sentence, I'd be out of a job and back on the street anyway. I'm just saving myself the effort.

Here is my last good reason to stay in detention until even the stubby little yellow afterschool buses have taken the rich kids home from practice. It's cold outside, and our house has broken windows.

I don't know where I want to be today. Not here, but not anywhere else either.

Thursday, October 21

Tod, please don't crack your gum today while you write. It's annoying. The echo is very loud in this empty room, and it always startles me. Thank you.

Hey, I'll try to be quieter with the gum. Chewing and cracking gum stops me from sticking out my tongue when I write.

Gum cracking also gives me a feeling like I'm still alive. But my friends aren't so sure. They think I'm being brainwashed. They have heard stories of guys like me who lose it all after a few weeks under these crappy fluorescent lights. They expect the system will sap the sheer willpower that keeps my kind of personality alive in this detergent box. My loyal garbage-picking droogs think I'm getting my sharp edges removed by you in some weird mind game that is being played on me. Maybe the gum is my only defense here in jail. It keeps my guard off guard.

On the other hand, there is definitely something to be said

for freedom. You told me that delivering a certain number of words is the key to freedom. So, please let me explain here and now that today I am absolutely going to fill up the number of words I write upon these pages by using a lot of synonyms. That trick is exactly the same one that is used by rich people like lawyers and advertising people when they want to charge more for their advice. If I use a lot of short synonyms and adjectives and strings of similar words then I can be out of this delightful, beautiful, pleasant, joyful, garden-like room before the sun goes down on this lousy, gray, cold, depressing, crappy, terrible, ugly, meaningless, rotten, hurtful, lousy, miserable cold day. Also, I intend to fill and fill and fill these pages by using short words when I happen to know that it is a fact that you want me to be revving up my twelve-cylinder brain and not pushing it down the street like some homeless dude with an overloaded grocery cart looking like he raided a Salvation Army dumpster.

[That is an atrocious mixed metaphor, and I'm not even sure what you mean.]

Short words that don't describe school: hard, tough, good, fun, smart, nice, kind, fair.

Short words that do describe school: cold, empty, wasted, lonely, rude, lost, unfair, weird, dumb, awful, awfuller, awfullest.

Some longer words: competitive, disadvantaged, confrontational, valueless, forgettable, Neanderthal, dysfunctional, incarceration.

Do you like my jumbo handwriting? Today you won't need those little reading glasses you wear on that chain. You can read this from across the room.

That's it. Time's up. Hand in your notebook. Time to go home.

Friday, October 22

Tod, good afternoon. I can see that the honor system isn't working for you, at least not with your journal pages. I've got to thank you; counting words had become a little tedious for me, too. From now on, we'll be counting how many pages you fill instead. And the inch-high letters do make your handwriting a lot easier to read, but let's stick between the lines, okay?

Why don't you write about your friends today—the ones who are downstairs in detention, cleaning the school grounds right now? Who are they, where did you meet them, and so on? I see that you call them your "droogs." In the book A Clockwork Orange, *the narrator's droogs are his partners in crime rather than his friends. Is that how you see your gang, Tod?*

First of all, no fair changing the rules.

Second of all, *gang* is a loaded word. Gangs wear colors. Gangs have initiations. I doubt sharing Cheetos and Coke on a couch counts as an initiation. We're not out doing Jets and

Sharks on the street. We're just outcasts who don't like authority. Mostly we spend our time wasting time until something actually happens around here.

And last of all, no. No way. I'm not interested in picking apart my pals, my buds, my droogs, just so you can get a peek inside.

I've got a better idea how to use up all the extra pages you gave me. I'm going to aim my laser eye on this fine institution you help run. You're my direct line to the top, and I've got plenty to say. Finally, someone's going to listen. Maybe we'll get some changes around here. There are a lot of mindless decisions made at this school that nobody—I mean nobody—can explain.

Here's one. Why does the school day start officially at 7:35? Why not 7:30 or 7:45 or a time you could remember? Why not 7:41 or, even better, a nice round 10:00? I'm sure school ends at 2:55 for the same reason. And that's not all. On teacher conference days, we get out precisely 37 minutes early. I'm definitely not complaining about the shorter classes. But with numbers like these, you've got to wonder about who's running things. And these are just the decisions you can see right away. I can only imagine what other stupidity is lurking where the students aren't allowed.

Now I get to the other insanity: lunchtime. It's no secret that lunch is my favorite time of the school day. Hell, it's anybody's favorite time, not just a fat boy's. Four days a week we have lunch at 11:04, except on those short days when it's 10:17. Lunch at 10:17? Who eats lunch when most normal people haven't even had breakfast yet? On weekends, or when I'm busy being suspended, I'm still breathing pillow that early.

And speaking of weekends, I can have weekend breakfast any time I want. That's because I'm lucky. My mom isn't the perfect TV mom bugging me to get up just because the organic eggs and sausages are ready before tennis lessons. She doesn't care when I eat, just so long as I don't go into her cupboard or her shelf in the fridge. Weekend breakfasts come out of huge boxes of frosted cereal from the warehouse club. Sometimes there's milk. And the side of the box says there are oats in the cereal, so it's good for you. On school days my mom won't pay for my breakfast. She makes me grab the free hot breakfast at school, which I hate.

Things don't really change much from day to day. The bell rings, and I stretch and yawn after the world's slowest science class. I've got one of the blind inclusion kids for my science partner. It's really weird, I have to say stuff like "don't drop that" or "the potion is turning green" and help him touch inside the opened-up frog. Blind Stuart doesn't care how dorky he looks, he touches everything and giggles. Then he comes in the next day with these really good typed-up notes and gives me a copy. He always gets it right. So that's Science.

I always do all my homework right here in Study Hall, unless there's a paper that needs research or something. Homework here is such a joke, you can do it all in class or in Study Hall. But nobody does it. They just talk.

And then there's good old lunchtime. That's the best. A

lot of kids hurry right up to the hot lunch line. I'm usually the last guy to get hot lunch. I guess the main reason is because these idiots are gorging themselves way early in the morning and they're going to be starving by the time school lets out. I guess if they've got the spare coin to buy candy and soda from the machines, they've got an edge. It's risky for me. Sometimes a chump will lend me pocket change for a candy bar, but that's getting unpredictable. Lately I prefer not to snack between meals. Why waste money in vending machines when stores leave the candy out in the open, where you can pick the piece you want. And when you're last in line in the cafeteria, maybe you get a bigger serving of what's left. Nobody's watching them punch your free-lunch card either.

I think the main reason I wait to eat is because my pals and I have a regular card game. We play euchre, because it takes brains and teamwork and nobody else plays it. It only takes two or three minutes for all of us to be present and accounted for. We sit in the same four seats at the same table in the same corner of the lunchroom every day, right between the blind kids and the stoners. I stop the game five minutes before lunch ends. That's when I get in the lunch line.

The rules are simple. First one gets the corner seat. It's got a perfect view of the entire lunchroom. Nobody can sneak up and sucker punch you or box your ears when you're in the corner. Then it goes clockwise. Second person sits to the left, third is across from second, and last is across from me. I'm usually first at the table because my locker is closest to the cafeteria. Partners sit diagonally. This setup means we don't get into fights about teams. It also means nobody has the same partner every day and figures out ways of cheating.

The other day, I was first and Rex came next. He dumped a magazine on the table and swung his legs over the seat. "Hey, Pops," he said to me. "I could sure use a dollar."

"I'm sure you could," I shot back, "and I could use a hundred. But we live with what we've got."

"Aw, c'mon, Munn. You know I don't get no lunch," he grumbled.

"You keep selling your free lunch cards, Rex."

Rex grabbed his magazine and rolled it up. He used it like a telescope, scanning the room slowly for extra food to beg, borrow, or whatever.

"Greg's over there with his movie buddies."

"You see anything?" I asked.

"Nope. They think they're so smart."

"They *are* smart, Rex. That's the problem."

While Pirate Rex searched the seas for abandoned lunches, Rob and Bernie sat down with their bag lunches and were just as totally predictable as Rex.

You've got little Bernie stuffing his grinning face with egg salad, which he eats at least 360 days a year. Bernie's even worse off than me at home. But he's always happy, always chippy or chipper or whatever the word is. He's the one who usually lays out some peacekeeping lines to keep Rex and me from scrabbling, something like, "C'mon guys, let's just play cards." I think Bernie's got no idea he's poor. He wouldn't hurt anybody, not that he could, and he's always got my back. I've known Bernie the longest.

Rob is a whole different story. He gives us a bit of class. Middle class. He's got braces and a normal boring family and only his dad has to work. Rob's headed straight to hell on the road called college. He's all smiles, all laughs, all make-believe. Rob gets an allowance but it's never enough for him. That's probably why he's with us instead of the other privileged kids like Greg. Rob's a kid you watch out for when he stops smiling.

Back to Rex. He's unpredictable. I mean, he's okay when he doesn't want something from you. Rex can be pretty funny when he's goofing on somebody. But I'm one of the few people who can manage his moods. He's not anybody's idea of a student, either. Rex takes mostly shop classes. He'll probably fix cars like his dad, but I bet he can't run his own garage. Rex looks at you with kind of glassy eyes. His mom drinks and it probably messed him up in her belly. Even worse, his missing teeth make him look stupid.

And these are my friends, in case you were wondering.

I'd be perfectly happy to describe how to play euchre, but I've definitely filled all my pages for today. I will say, before I hit the road, that I figured out something important during the game one day. You know how you always wish you said the right thing at the right time? Some kid came over to watch us play and asked us the rules. I told him euchre is like life, because if you don't know the rules, you have no idea how to play. That's exactly what I said, too.

Tuesday, October 26

Tod, would you please tell me in your own words what happened yesterday?

Well, you're the guidance counselor. I'm sure you're all up to date on why I didn't come to detention yesterday. Don't they post a Most Wanted list in the coffee room? I guess you're like the rest of us, and you crave an action-packed, well-written story. I'll tell you one thing. I didn't care about missing our detention party or anything. I didn't really care about one less day of writing my arm off in a big empty room. I didn't care about slugging another dweeb with loafers and a hairstyle. I didn't care about going home, either. But Mr. Principal Carnegie didn't have to call my mom, and even if he did have to call my mom, he didn't have to make her come get me. I'm a big boy. I can get home all by myself.

Mom already had a massive pile of mending to do. Mrs. Tagliapietra at the dry cleaners has been breathing down Mom's neck to mend people's suits and shirts and skirts faster and faster, in record time, like she's appointed herself Mom's coach for an Olympic sewing event. Mom could win on her own, I bet. And Mom certainly didn't need Carnegie to tell her that I'm a thug and a delinquent and have no right to be among the civilized elite. She knows it. But what's the point of getting her all riled up before she comes on the bus to get me? What's she going to do, show up and put a leash and muzzle on me in the principal's office to show that she's in control or something?

No, Mom's got her own way of doing things. Mom walked into Carnegie's office and just glared at me. The secretary asked her a few times to sign the clipboard with the sign-in sheet, but my mother wasn't on a listening tour. I was slumping down on the wooden bench with my hands in my sweatshirt pocket. My legs were sticking out straight in the aisle, ready to trip somebody by accident. I'd been looking out the window until she came in. Then she gave me the silent evil eye, and I was suddenly a lot more interested in the tops of my shoes.

She still had her pincushion on. I mean, clipped to her lapel, she still had her little fake-tomato pincushion, a porcupine filled with needles and pearl-headed pins that moved up and down with her hard breathing. I studied my purple shoelace on the left and my black shoelace on the right with equal interest, waiting, waiting, waiting for Mom to make a sound. The secretary tried asking Mom to sign in for about the fifth time, but Mom just dismissed her with a backhand wave. That was the only sign of life from Mom—the heaving pincushion and the short royal wave. Otherwise, she was like one of those silent movie magicians who try to send a psychic message across the theater by being really intense with her bugging-out eyes. Finally I cocked my head in Mom's direction and caught her eye for only a brief second. That was enough to get her going. She lost her cool and grabbed at me, grabbed at the collar of my shirt and tried yanking me up off that old bench. You know what happened next. I was still sitting, and Mom had one more sewing job ahead of her. I didn't really care anyway about the shirt. Somebody had dropped it off at Mrs. Tagliapietra's and didn't ever pick it up. Looking at the soupy green color, with the ugly embroidered horse on the pocket, it's easy to see why it was abandoned.

At the sound of the ripping shirt, who do you think was standing in the doorway watching this tender mothering moment? Nobody but Herr Principal Carnegie. He started to speak.

"Don't you think . . ." he said. And then he stopped. He took one look at my mom holding my ripped shirt collar, with her cheap dress and weird stuffed tomato pincushion brooch and no stockings and varicose veins, and boy could I read his mind. He realized that he was too smart to waste his time educating lowlifes. (Lowlives?) Especially lowlife punks with lowlife moms who don't dress up better to yank their kids out of school. He made some kind of nodding eye contact with the secretary, then stepped back and closed his door quietly. The latch clicked like a small prison door being secured, and it made me jump. Not because I was scared. I didn't care, at least not about Carnegie's idea of my career path. I cared about a long, long bus ride home with Mom.

I pulled myself forward off the bench. She handed me my collar like it was a lethal injection. I turned toward the door and felt a familiar sharp jab between my shoulder blades—the jab of the palm of a hand pushed hard by an angry short woman. Maybe the muzzle and leash were on after all.

Wednesday, October 27 (continued)

Tod, please do not rip pages from this notebook anymore. I promise that anything you write will remain only between you and me, but anything you write must also stay in this book. I won't judge or punish you for your actions if you describe them honestly. After you handed up your notebook yesterday, I discovered the torn pages in the trash can—the pages in which you describe tormenting poor Ricardo Manzana yesterday and breaking his glasses. You'll find those pages stapled inside the front cover of this notebook, where I want them to stay. I have left the rest of your entry here.

By the way, you're doing a nice job of description.

hall just as the final bell for sixth period rang. I was kicking myself for being late—I shouldn't have stopped for Ricardo. I should have discussed our business arrangements in the lunchroom. Even if I'm late to other classes, I have to be on time for Mr. Harmon's class because that was the deal I made with myself. And I don't go back on deals.

I broke into a run, and that was a mistake. Not because the Hallway Police might write me up, but because I ran by a couple of girls closing their lockers.

"Someone doesn't want to be tardy," said the girl with the pleated skirt. It was Karen Dominick. She always smells great.

The other one, Paula Something, looked shrunk in her

boyfriend's football team jacket. "It's too late. He was *born* tardy!"

While these two geniuses nearly choked themselves laughing, I came up to my classroom door. Next to the door, Mr. Harmon has taped up pictures of a bunch of writers with their quotes popping out of their mouths in cartoon balloons. It's stupid, but I always stop and read the stuff these dead guys had to say about writing and thinking. I can remember them all. Here's the one from Ben Franklin, who I like. Whom I like?

[Whom—the action is being done to him.]

Anyway, Ben Franklin was a pretty smart guy and his family didn't have any money when he was growing up.

If you would not be forgotten,
As soon as you are dead and rotten,
Either write things worth reading,
Or do things worth the writing.

I can see why a teacher would stick that on a door. It would probably be on a lot more doors in a lot more schools if other teachers tried putting up cool quotes like Mr. Harmon does.

Once I pulled open the door, I could see that I hadn't missed anything. The bell had rung, but Mr. Harmon was standing by his desk joking with a flock of girls about a TV show they all watch. It was like a party up there. They were repeating lines from the show and bursting into laughter. I could tell the girls like him because he's got a goatee beard and expensive glasses and he drives a save-the-earth car. He doesn't even talk like he went to one of those overnight schools where you wear uniforms and you only see your parents on Christmas. I don't know why he's wasting his time at this dump. Maybe he has to do some kind of community service or something. The girls kept staring and smiling and shifting their weight from one leg to another like dancers.

So I closed the door and it clicked and that busted the magic party bubble. Mr. Harmon's eyes shot up to the clock, then he clapped his hands together and told everybody to take a seat. Meanwhile, his fan club decided I'd wrecked their fun and shot me looks to kill. That's why they call these girls drop-dead gorgeous—if they're gorgeous, they want you to drop dead. Karen Dominick came in after I did, but the only person who gave her dirty looks was Dandruff Derek. No surprise there. He gives dirty looks to all the girls.

I just lowered my head and got a seat almost all the way in the back. Mr. Harmon is friendly enough but he gets right down to business. "All right, let's start with the homework. Raise your hand if you're handing it in, hide your face if you're not." Then he walked around the room taking papers, making comments the whole time.

"Thank you. And you. And you. But *not* you. Or you, again. Hey, Charlene, you got one in on time! Congratulations! Nothing again, Zab? Your dog must be pretty sick of the taste of homework. Tod, as always, the handwriting hides what's inside." And so on. It seems like he almost always calls out some compliment when it's my turn. Too bad everybody pretends not to notice. I guess they're jealous. It's not exactly hard to read a book and write an opinion. All you need is an opinion.

Mr. Harmon stood in front of the blackboard looking like he was up to something. He put on his glasses. He tucked his shirt collar back into his sweater vest and shuffled through our papers. "Hmm. Who's my victim going to be?" he said with a little grin. "Who wants to tell the class about man's inhumanity to man as represented in Orwell's *Animal Farm*?"

It sounded like the whole class moaned when he said this. Either you like to speak in front of people or you can put it on paper. I've met a lot of kids who can't do either, but I haven't met anyone who can do both. No, wait a minute. Kevin Stanofsky talks and writes like he's on the TV news. He always makes pretty funny comments in class, and he's got this perfect haircut all the time. After Mr. Harmon goes fishing for someone to say something intelligent and comes up empty, he calls on Kevin. He's running for class treasurer, too. Kevin, I mean.

But Kevin wasn't here today. He was probably out putting up another couple thousand election posters in the cafeteria. (With all those color copies, it makes you think twice about making him treasurer.) Mr. Harmon was still glancing over our homework papers, the few he had, but he knows better than to call on me. Every time he tries it, I do Stupid Tod.

I'm probably not as stupid as Stupid Tod, but I don't want to let my so-called peers peer inside my brain. I remember what Marlon Brando told Sonny in *The Godfather* . . . never let them know what you're thinking. Brando was smart enough to run an underworld syndicate, so I follow his advice.

"Greg?"

I don't remember what Greg said, but it wasn't worth remembering and definitely not worth writing down here. Mr. Harmon shuffled through a couple more papers. Then he stopped forever to read a crumpled one.

"Tod?"

Oh, jeez. Not me. Now I had to put on the lobotomy helmet and face the world. First thing I do is roll my eyes.

"Huh?" I muttered.

"Come on, Tod. Pretend you speak the way you write."

I decided to look at the window. At it, but not through it. "Um, what was the question?" I said. This got more laughs from the idiots than Stanofsky gets on his best day.

"Man's inhumanity to man. Or, in this case, animal's inanimality to animals. So why do people treat other people badly, Tod? Use an example from Orwell's *Animal Farm* to support your answer. Just tell us what you wrote."

"He knows all about inanimality to animals," said some girl. More yuks all around.

"Munn-ster!" said whichever guy wanted to be her boyfriend the most.

"Everybody zip it up," said Mr. Harmon. He looked around and he wasn't smiling. "Raise your hand if you didn't hand in your paper." More squinty-eyed stares and glazed gazes. "I see some of you forgot that you forgot your homework. So if you don't mind, we'll just hear from someone who remembered. Tod?"

Oh, God, this wasn't going to end at all, was it? I hate this part. I can talk to my friends, or to cops, and sound perfectly innocent. I can talk to store clerks about Mother's Day cards while my friends steal. But I can't talk in class. Or to girls. But Mr. Harmon seemed like he wasn't letting go.

"Tod . . . why do you think the pigs ultimately turn on each other?"

I waited a little. I coughed into my hand. I sniffed. I snorted. Then I looked Mr. Harmon in the eye and decided to hell with it and finally said, "Because that's what you do in the jungle, the farm, whatever. You take care of yourself. These pigs, Snowball, Napoleon, they needed each other to get control of the farm."

Mr. Harmon's face brightened. "Go on."

All right, but just this once.

"But when they got the keys to the farm, they didn't need each other anymore, right? So what do you expect them to do? They did what everyone out there does."

"Excellent. Excellent," said Mr. Harmon. "And what's that?"

I didn't get to answer because the door opened. One of the sentries popped his head in and said my name like he was ordering a sandwich. He scanned the room and caught me before I could look away. I was too busy talking to think straight. He walked right down the aisle with his keys and metal stuff jangling. I pretty much stood right up. These guys may wear brown uniforms, but they're just like regular policemen. They have guns.

"Grab your bag. Let's go."

Suddenly, Mr. Harmon leapt over a desk. He threw himself onto the sentry and wrestled away the gun. "You stupid idiot! How dare you? This is my star pupil!" screamed Mr. Harmon, putting the rent-a-cop into a choke hold. The sentry struggled, but Mr. Harmon creamed him with a dictionary until he was unconscious. Then my teacher wiped his shoes on the sentry's uniform and smiled at me. "Go on with your brilliant essay, Tod," he said, beaming uncontrollably. "Educate this class full of morons."

Yup. That's what happened, except for one small difference. I left out the part where Mr. Harmon stood speechless while I shuffled out of the room with the cop behind me. I didn't look at Mr. Harmon at all. I didn't have to.

"Guess who's gonna pay for that kid's glasses you busted?" said my armed guard, real loud, before he kicked the door closed with a very shiny black shoe.

I've already told you about the part where my mom got called. It's funny that I didn't get kicked out of school. Just my mom getting called and an early dismissal. I still can't figure out why. Did you have anything to do with that?

Thursday, October 28

Tod, before you start today, please read the note I wrote at the top of your journal entry yesterday. Except for tearing out your pages, you're being a lot more cooperative about writing than you were during the first few days. Thank you. Today, I'd appreciate it if you would tell me a little more about your home and family. If that isn't too intrusive.

Intrusive? Nah. My sainted grandmother always said that if your guidance counselor warden wants to be your shrink, let her. My mother, however, says that if I cause any more trouble, she'll make the decisions you people are afraid to make. She means it. You want cooperation? Here's cooperation. You want to peek in my window? Here's this morning's excitement. Hang on to your seat.

Bernie was at my house way too early. He doesn't live far from me, just on the street behind mine. Most people walk around the block when paying a call to our mansion, but Bernie always cuts through a couple of yards and pushes his scrawny, short self through the busted slat in my neighbor's fence. I used to be able to pop through that triangle when I was seven or eight, but that was many cheeseburgers ago.

I've told Insomniac Bernie a couple thousand times that Rule Number One on a school morning is: "Don't loom outside my room." Today I could hear him crunching around in the leaves and high grass outside my window, pacing back and forth. He's like a puppy waiting for the ball to get thrown. You know those hyper little sidekicks in the movies who buzz around the big honcho and always smile? That's Bernie. Scrunch, scrunch, hop, hop, dancing in the leaves. It sounded like he was pouring cold cereal from a dump truck.

"Bernie!" I shouted with my head still in the pillow. "Get lost."

"C'mon, Tod. Open the door!" Like all shrimps, Bernie has a buzzy, whiny voice. "You're not going to believe this."

"Forget it. Bus doesn't come for twenty minutes." Mornings, my head is like a cement block on the pillow. Even feels the same shape.

"I found something cool. Too cool," said Bernie.

I could hear him well—too well—because our wooden walls are thin and rickety. Also, I've got some cardboard where a window pane used to be. It's supposed to keep out the draft.

"Fourteen minutes. Count 'em. Then come back," I muttered.

He was still circling under my window. My room is on the first floor, mainly because my entire house is on the first floor. Kids at my school have bigger garages than our whole house.

"Did your mom fix my coat?" he asked.

Oh, right. His winter coat. He wasn't wearing a coat. Bernie had to be freezing out there.

"Yeah, the rip. Fixed the rip. Hold on," I yelled. I had to act fast before he started a fire alongside the house to keep warm. Seriously.

"Just give me a second," I called.

Suddenly the wall of my bedroom started to shake with short explosions. Fists.

"Middle of the night! Shut the hell up!" *Bang, bang, bang!*

That was Dick, my mother's husband. Is he ever. He was making my authentic imported James Bond poster flutter on the plywood wall. "You hear me?" he threatened.

I knew better than to yell back how 6:41 a.m. wasn't the middle of the night. It was actually the far end, also known as "the morning." But for all I knew, it was the middle of Dick's night. Or the beginning. He's no way predictable, except in his low opinion of me.

I reached under my bed and pulled out Bernie's coat, right where I'd left it. I bit off a thread that was still hanging where the rip was fixed. Then I ran out of my room, which is in the front of our splendid four-room house. I sleep in what used to be the front porch. There's nothing but squares of glass in the top half of the two outside walls. Long ago it was glassed in by someone who thought winter breezes and summer sunstroke were good for you. My mom and dad moved us into the house when I was pretty small. The Crystal Palace has always been my room.

On early winter nights like these, I sleep in more clothes than I wear to school. So I didn't have to get dressed to open the locks and haul Bernie into the front room. He was swimming in two sweaters, and he had a river of snot running from his pointy little nose. He pulled his backpack off one shoulder and started digging into it. It's red, and the rips are held together with safety pins.

"Bernie, it's the middle of the night. Come back in eleven minutes."

He fished out a blue and orange rectangle of paper and slid it into my hand. "Check it out, Pops. You're on a Chinese menu."

"Hot and Sour," I said, not looking, not listening. I handed it back to him. "Give me a minute to brush my teeth."

"Keep it DOWN out there!" yelled Dick. Bernie and I just ignored him. When I got back out of the bathroom, I peeled off a sweatshirt and was ready to go. No need to change clothes. These were them. Free hot breakfast is served at school for us lucky folks whose moms lock up the Lucky Charms on schooldays.

"Let's go."

"It's really cold, Tod. Did your mom fix my coat?"

I pretended like I didn't know. "Well, she might have. If she did, it would be on the coat chair." We don't have a front hall closet. We have a chair by the door.

"Aw, man. Can you look?"

Suddenly I looked surprised. "Hey! Here it is!" I went over to the overloaded coat chair and peeled back all the clothes I had just piled onto Bernie's coat. Like Houdini yanking a tablecloth under a meal, I pulled out my latest masterpiece. He snatched it up and checked the stitching around the rip.

Bernie giggled as quietly as he could. He put the coat on over his sweaters and we headed to the sidewalk. Our front door has five locks on it. I only have one key. I didn't lock any. Why should I?

"Wow, nice job," he said. "Thank your mom for me. My mom would have done it, but . . ."

"Yeah, I'll thank her," I interrupted, sucking the cold October air into my lungs and trying to gargle it. "But don't you talk to her about it. She gets all weird about free jobs, especially when she knows you ripped it jumping a fence."

"You told her about Gilley's dog?" Mr. Gilley is a nasty man, and his dog is a nasty German shepherd. Both of them used to work in a department store at night. One of them was caught stealing. Now that puppy guards a tool shed where similar goodies can sometimes be found. At night. When the dog is asleep. Which he wasn't.

I just stared at Bernie until he realized I wasn't serious. We reached the bus stop soon enough.

"C'mon, Pops," said Bernie. "Look at this Chinese menu."

"Are you still on about that? Forget it. It's too dark to read anyway."

"I'll light my shiny silver lighter."

"Hell you will. Keep your flamethrower away from me. I can read it just fine." I snatched the menu out of his hand and gave it an actual look.

"Town Thai restaurant?"

"Yeah," he said, beaming.

"Bernie, do you have any idea where Thailand is?"

He shrugged. "China, right?" He couldn't care less.

"Sure," I said. It's easier to do Bernie's homework myself than try to teach him something. All he cares about is cars and motorcycles and playing with his lighter. Except he didn't have anything to do with the fire in the stairs last month. Honest.

[I'll take your word for it.]

I opened the Thai menu and took a look again. I'll give this to Bernie. It sure looked like a Chinese menu. This was some dumb joke of his. Then Bernie pulled off a thin glove and pointed to the Appetizers column. I read it.

Tod Mun Koong
The popular Thai-style shrimp cake served with
pungent sauce and crushed peanuts

Pungent, sure. Crushed, my enemies will be. Popular, never.

"I found it blowing down the street yesterday," said Bernie. "Dunno why, but I decided to read it. You can keep it."

Great, I thought. A menu for another restaurant I can't ever go to. I'll put it in the suitcase I never use.

Someday I'll have enough money. Someday I'll actually get to keep the money Mom makes when I'm doing her easy mending. She told Dick that a grunt like me needs some kind of skill to keep out of jail. Mom enrolled me in her sewing trade school but she didn't ask my permission. She doesn't pay me, either. She says she pays me with food and clothes and shelter.

When I think about the accommodations, I decide I'm getting a raw deal.

Sewing's easy. It's chimp work. I can do it, but I wouldn't admit it. And I get absolutely no satisfaction watching Bernie run his fingers along my fine, fine stitching.

"Yeah," said Bernie with a satisfied sigh as we plopped down on the overheated bus. "Your mom did a real good job on my coat."

Friday, October 29

Repairing your friend's coat was a good deed. It sounds like you enjoy doing positive things for people. Would you care to write down more accounts like that?

You're making this too easy, Mrs. W. Soon you'll be asking me to bring you an apple and write Mother's Day cards.

Here's a good deed I did, okay? This afternoon I was walking near the main entrance on my way to the lunchroom. I was just minding my own business when I heard a girl around the corner say "Whoa!" really loudly. I started toward the front doors to see what was happening. Just before I reached the corner, a stapler came flying past my ear and nearly beaned me. I stopped, but the stapler didn't. It clattered across the floor, past the metal detector, until it smacked into the stupid Honor Roll case.

"Watch out!" said the girl, and immediately she bugged me. First of all, she said "watch out" *after* she tried to kill me, and second, she said it like I was doing something to *her*. I rounded the corner in a bad mood and nearly bumped into a stepladder. Standing on the very top of the ladder—on top of the sticker that says, "Danger! Don't Stand Here!"—was that spooky goth girl Luz Montoya.

This is the part where I'm supposed to describe her. Why should I? She's a spooky goth girl and everyone knows her. She dresses like a vampire. She wears makeup like a corpse. She flits around the hall with her big flat portfolio case instead of a backpack, as if her next class is always art class. Well, I'm in her art class, and I'll tell you this—she always sings. And she sings in the hallways. Not good songs or even recognizable songs. Her songs always sound important, but I've listened to them, and they're meaningless. I'm totally convinced they're show tunes.

About that good deed. Instead of heading to lunch like a smart guy would, or cussing her out like a wise guy should, I handed her back her stapler. She hardly barely even thanked me. So I walked around the ladder looking to read her big old banner. But I couldn't make any sense of it. It was painted with a desert scene. You know—camels and pyramids and so on. No sphinx.

"Why are you stapling Egypt to the wall?" I asked her. But she just pulled the top of the stapler away from the bottom and pounded it mercilessly against her mural.

"You got staples," she asked. Kind of asked. Told me, really. "I'm almost out."

"Why'n hell would I have staples?"

"I dunno. You seem like you always have a bunch of stuff."

I couldn't figure out if she meant that as an insult or a compliment. She was really smacking that stapler hard.

"No," I said, "no staples. No nails or glue or tacks. No Velcro."

"What about electrical tape?" she added, leaning way over the wall clock.

"No library paste either. You're gonna fall if you keep that up."

"Yeah? Well, I'm a panther."

I had NO idea what she meant. "I've never heard of a panther that survived a ladder accident," I told her, trying to sound statistical.

She came right back with a comment. "You don't read the right newspapers."

"Maybe not," I said, "but my mom's an E.R. nurse and she says a lot of people crack their skulls on ladders for being too cocky."

"Maybe," she said, "but your mom does sewing for the dry cleaner's over on Garson Avenue."

I was done with my good deed. She had her stapler. It was time for lunch.

I was seriously hungry when I hit the lunchroom. The smell of the sloppy joes clouded my mind. I didn't want to wait to the end of the period to eat. I didn't want to wait in line, either. I just scoped the front of the lunch line for someone to let me in.

It didn't look good at first. All I saw were jocks and snitches and girls. You've got to be careful when you're on probation. Just when it looked like I'd have to be number fifty in line, shrimpy Tony Constantino magically appeared up front, looking really eager to help me. Actually, he was busy mooning like a starving man at curvy Karen Dominick and her black sweater. Then Tony felt my eyes on his back. He jolted and turned his head my way as he picked up a tray. Too bad for Tony, who knows the drill. He handed me the tray and his place in line. He hovered behind me, hoping the kids behind *him* would have mercy. No way. I could hear the chorus singing behind us.

"Hey, Tony, why'd you let that freak in?"

"One of you losers, hit the back of the line."

"You cave, you starve, Tony."

"Them's the rules."

My host Tony faded out of line and vanished while I took his place in the doorway. The grumbling stopped, except for the sneer on the face of Nardine, the hairnet-wearing old lunch lady who watched my grand entrance. To make her point, Nardine gave the vat of sloppy joes two or three stabs with her ice cream scoop before glopping some meat onto the bun. She held out the cardboard plate with her surgery gloves like she was holding something disgusting. On most days she usually was, but not today.

"More," I said, locking eyes with her.

"What?" she asked, as if she'd never seen a hungry person before. "Take the plate."

"That's not enough food."

"That's all you get."

"Please, sir, I'd like some more," I said, not blinking, voice even. I was trying not to sound sarcastic.

"You move on," warned Nardine

"More. Sloppy. Joe. Now."

"You don't need no more food. You need to lose some fat, stop picking on kids, get yourself a damn haircut. You should starve."

"Hey, Munn, move on," sneered a jock. "Or else."

I didn't stop looking at my lady friend behind the counter. I didn't take the plate back, either. I just stood statue-still. The jock and some other kids started shoving me, trying to get their arms around the doorway. I changed position, locked my legs, and stuck my big feet against the steam table to hold my ground. They piled up, with arms and legs waving, yelling at each other to cut out the shoving. But I didn't budge.

"Just slop the pig, lady. Give him mine. Give him the whole vat. Who cares? Just get him out of here."

Nardine opened her mouth and shot me something like a smile. A smile from a jack-o-lantern. It was something I could respect. It was pure nastiness.

"The only reason I'm giving you more," Nardine muttered, hurling gobs of saucy meat onto every part of the plate, "is because I know what's in it. I can only hope it kills you."

The added weight of the sloppy joe nearly snapped my wrist. I stepped aside and the kids behind me tumbled. I don't know if any of them fell down or not, but they screamed like they'd fallen into lava. I can't say I cared. I was too busy getting my free lunch card punched.

Monday, November 1

Tod, today you were observed pressuring a student for money. Since the student refused and you didn't retaliate, you were not reprimanded. Why, Tod? Does that make any sense?

A lot of things in this school don't make sense. The windows don't open. The doors don't close. They cancel the Halloween party every year. But I don't have nearly the patience to write down the whole list. Today I'll just jump to the least sensible, most ridiculous, barely tolerable aspect of school. It's called art class.

Okay, I get that math and science are important. Like breathing and eating, you can't avoid them. No matter where you go, you're stuck with plants and volcanoes and blood cells and numbers and variables that can be multiplied and square-rooted. Fine. Got to learn it or die trying, right?

But art class is painful, treacherous, meaningless, and just unjust. It is worse than a waste of time. It crushes the human spirit. At this very moment you are probably wondering what I am talking about.

[I am.]

Here are two perfect examples. Two weeks ago, Phister had us sketch the perfect house for a project in class. Okay. So I drew a perfect house. *My* perfect house. It was on Mount Everest, with a huge wall around it. There were guards and laser cannons on each corner. The main drawbridge was raised over a wide trench of electrified mutant piranhas. Plus, it had its own heliport. I got a D.

Why should this guy get to mess up my grades with his loser opinions? I thought the point of art class was to pick out a few Picassos and let the rest of us relax between real classes. So I asked Phister why I got a D, and he said something about perspective and shading. I said I was expressing myself freely using the medium of ink. He said I doodled bad comic book garbage with a ballpoint pen and I shouldn't have used the good paper. I asked him if he meant the paper for the good students and he actually said yes, that was exactly what he meant, there wasn't enough to waste.

Then I asked him what it would take to get an A, and he said a real house and a real imagination. I said I'd figure that one out and get back to him. So that explains the D, okay?

Here's the other example. That girl Luz with the stapler was part of a new thing Phister came up with. The Artist of the Month. He told us about it in class today. He said she's not technically in our art class, she's in what he calls his "workshop class," which is at the exact same time in the exact same room.

Phister showed us some of her paintings. There was a school bus shaped like a pyramid in the desert, and a mummy's painted case with a regular, normal woman inside reading the newspaper. They were kind of funny. She's definitely the person who's been putting the stickers with the sphinx wearing sunglasses on all the stop signs near the school.

According to Phister, that girl Luz's masterpiece is—you guessed it—something Egyptian. It's a statue of a sphinx. Now, a sphinx is supposed to have the head of a man and the body of a lion, right? No, not hers. Our lucky Art of the Month is a statue with a head like the sphinx and the body of . . . something else.

"What? What?" we all asked breathlessly. "What is the body of the Art of the Month? We *have* to know!" Some of the girls fainted with excitement. Yeah, right.

Then he told us to go down to the main entrance and see it. Phister said it was what real talent was all about.

Now this freaky girl was starting to make sense. The big jewelry and the dark clothes and the fat black eyeliner . . . she's not playing goth. She's playing Egyptian.

A bunch of kids said they were going right away to the front door to see the statue. What dorks. They're going to pass it twice a day for a month. What's the hurry? It's not like I'm ever going to get one of my Ming vases up there on that pedestal.

The stupid thing is that I ended up in the entrance right after class anyway. It was supposed to snow today and I wanted to check out the front area and see if it was really going to be winter so soon. The same bunch of kids were clambering around the six-foot-high pedestal, looking up at her foot-high statue and the painted desert mural behind it. The Sahara. I think that's the name of it.

The statue was the sphinx all right, the same one without his nose that I've seen everywhere (except Egypt). He was pouncing in the same position as the usual sphinx, but his body was an old two-door sports car, an MG or Aston Martin like James Bond drove. The car had big fenders where the front legs usually are, and shiny silver hubcaps on the wheels. It looked real. Not like a real sphinx, but like a real artist made it. It was definitely a professional job. I guess it deserved to win. It's not like there's any competition.

Then I looked at the card on the base of the pedestal. It said, "Artist of the Month: Luz Montoya." She made the card fancy like the wall paintings inside a pyramid, with little sideways people and black birds and squiggly lines. She painted the background coffee brown, which made it look old.

Who wants their name printed fancy like that for everyone to see? A real artist. And she acts like one. The more important you treat yourself, the more you're worth.

That's what I figure, anyway.

Tuesday, November 2

Wow. No comment to start my notebook today. I guess I'm moving up in the world. At least I'm making progress here in the Fortress of Solitude.

[This can't be the Fortress of Solitude, Tod. There are two of us here. What might the word be? "Dualtude?"]

[I don't know. But I almost got through the day without a comment.]

Yesterday afternoon after I walked out of here, my droogs Rex and Rob were warming up in the front entrance of school. I could hear them grumbling from pretty far down the hall.

"Whyn't you bring gloves, you dipwit?" That was Rob.

"I lost them," said Rex.

Rob gave Rex that moan, the one that usually comes with a slap on the forehead. "You lost them, like, weeks ago."

"They're still lost. Give me yours and Mommy will buy you new ones."

"Like hell," said Rob. "I found these myself."

"I bet you found them," sniggered Rex. "Find me a pair. With rabbit or something inside."

"Will you two shut up?" I said, turning the corner. "You're screaming *private data* down the hall next to Evil Prince Ipple's office. Cripes."

Then I took a look at them. Rex had a runny nose and was blowing into his hands. Rob was scraping mud from the fat tread of his insulated hiking boots with a stick. Both of them were clearly cold, but Rob had the better deal. His winter parka was nice and cozy. On the other hand, Rex wore sneakers and his dad's scratchy checkered wool hunting jacket. The buttons were like wooden bowling pins tucked into loops. The jacket was huge on Rex because Rex's father is no small guy. I figured they'd be happy to see me.

"Where's Bernie?" I asked.

"Playtime over, Shakespeare?" asked Rob, not even looking up.

Rex fanned his chapped hands in my face, showing off a raw red callus under each finger. They'd been raking. "Hope you didn't hurt yourself yanking that big pencil." Rex guffawed like he'd said something funny.

"Yeah?" I muttered at Rex. "If you coulda kept your cool, we'd all be on Rob's couch watching cable TV instead of pushing wood around. You're lucky I'm a great writer."

Rob stood up straight and tossed his stick at the Egyptian Sculpture of the Month. It bounced off the mural behind the sculpture, leaving a clod of mud on a pyramid behind the sphinx. Rob sneered. "Will you listen to this crap? Pops, you're so full of it. You caught a break from the rake because you snitched or something."

"Snitched?"

"Something. You're up there writing confessions while we're on the chain gang. I'm the one she should have picked."

"Yeah, Rob? Why? 'Cause you've been on a plane? 'Cause you rode on a double-decker bus? 'Cause you've got a hundred video games? How exactly did you *get* those games, huh, Rob?"

"I didn't say that."

"You tough yet, Rob? You learn tough from us yet?"

"That's not what I meant. . . ."

Rob's voice ran out of gas like I thought it would. I didn't answer. I did my silent steaming thing instead, glowering at Rob. I let my eyes go wide and my jaw worked sideways like it was chewing a big wad of gum. That's what I think I look like when I lose my temper, and it's handy to fake it. I'm bigger than Rob in every direction and he knows it. He lowered his eyes.

In my pocket was a bunch of napkins because you never know if you're going to get a bloody nose by mistake. I balled up the napkins in my hand and pulled them out of my pocket. Now my big fist looked even bigger. Rex looked both ways down the hall. Rob stepped back toward the door and raised his palms.

"Now, listen, Pops . . ."

I didn't care what Rob had to say. I didn't want to hear it. I pulled back my arm. Rob flinched. Then I stepped right past Rob, reached up, and wiped the dumb mud off Cleopatra's Egyptian mural the best I could. I dabbed at it a few times and the crap mostly came off.

"Let's go to Rob's house and make fries in his oven," I said, tossing the muddy wadded napkins to Rob.

Rob cut a laugh of relief that sounded a little strained. But he got his smile back soon enough. He tries to be a slick salesman like his dad. "Nope. Forget it. It's Monday. My sister's Girl Scout troop. Ranger Mom's got them beading necklaces or something."

"Isn't it survival potholders this week?" asked Rex.

"Nope. Hairdo merit badges are next. If they ever do a march to a beauty shop, we can have the family room back."

"Where's Bernie?" I asked for the fifteenth time.

Rob was back to his full-on cocky smile now. "Bernie got called in from the office. They said he had a phone call. He didn't come back."

"You think it's his mom?" She's sick.

"I said I don't know," said Rob. "He didn't come back, remember?"

Bernie doesn't need any more crap in his life. "I bet it's his mom," I said. "Didn't she go and get an X-ray the other day?"

Rob rocked back on his heels. He started tapping the sides of his boots together to shake the last mud loose to the floor. "Jeez, Pops, why don't you call Bernie if you're keeping so up-to-date?"

"Look at dat floor!" Sudden irate janitor. "You pig get out. School closed." That how he talk.

I leaned back into the door and pushed the bar open with my butt. I walked out first, with my hands gripping the extra napkins to keep warm. The cold air bit my nose. I used to wear a scarf when I was a kid, but I wouldn't be caught dead in one now.

I looked back for a second, back to the school. The statue was blocked by the sticker that's stuck on every outside door.

NO TRESPASSING VIOLATORS

WILL BE PROSECUTED

Sometimes I wonder if they put that stupid sign on the wrong side of the door.

It was almost dark outside already. Now I had to go home to get food. There was nobody at the bus stop, which meant we'd just missed one. They run maybe every half hour. I think I'll go catch one right now.

[Tod, for the record, you can trust me any time you want to describe your "outside" activities. I will even repeat my promise of confidentiality. Nothing leaves this room. Why do your friends call you Pops?]

[Sorry.]

Wednesday, November 3

Still no comment to brighten my day? Well, I'm running out of things to write about.

I didn't really want to talk about this, but I guess I will. Not because this old story is supposed to be an excuse for the incident, okay? It has nothing to do with why we did what we did. And, most definitely, it's not an apology. It's just an old story.

So Bernie and I walked into the library after school about a month ago, just before Columbus Day. He was all hot to get his hands on the new copy of *Motorcycle Monthly*. Bernie wants to be a stunt rider in the movies when he gets older, if he ever gets a motorcycle. Whenever he pisses me off, I'm forced to remind him that the kids up on the hill already got bikes for their birthdays and they're busy practicing for the stunt rider jobs while he rots on his couch watching dirt bike rallies on TV. Last time I said that, Bernie surprised me with an actual comeback.

"Oh yeah?" he said with a snort. "Well, those rich kids aren't getting those jobs because their mommies won't let them do jumps and bruise their faces before their yearbook pictures get taken." Not bad for Bernie.

Bernie always bugs me about us hanging out at the school library. I don't know why he thinks it's weird. Where else am I going to get my books? At a bookstore? I'm already on the Ten Most Wanted list at every bookstore in walking distance of here. It's not my fault books are so expensive. A pad of paper is a dollar at the dollar store. Add a little ink and a cardboard cover and suddenly you've got to be rich to buy a book. Unless nobody wants the book. Then they take all the loser books and put them in a bin and they cost less than a blank pad of paper. I don't get it either.

At least somebody's tax money is paying for libraries. The public library seems to think I owe them $37 in overdue fees. Fat chance. But our school library isn't such a bad place, considering it's in our school.

Bernie wandered off to the magazine shelf and Mrs. Lent called me over.

The main librarian, Mrs. Lent, treats me pretty decently. She doesn't give me that crosswise look I get from Mrs. Culpepper every time I push past the turnstile. Mrs. Clodhopper does sweet things when I come up to check out a book, like put away the money box. That's right, she takes that little plastic file box with the slit on top and she shoves it in a drawer. It's never got more than two dollars in it, believe me, and it usually sits five feet behind the front desk. I think she really believes I'm going to leap over the desk and yank it from her fat hands. She's not exactly subtle.

At least Mrs. Lent treats me like I can read without my lips moving. Right after I transferred here, maybe it was the first day I came up to the library, I saw her name on the little sign and asked her if she married Mr. Lent so she could get a good librarian name. She gave me a nice smile and she calls me Tod and not Mr. Munn like that's some kind of insult. Lots of people think she's pretty strict but I think she's just misunderstood. And who wants to clean up after a bunch of losers who can't even put the books back where they belong?

Mrs. Lent gave me a worried look. "Tod, you're almost late for the bee," she said.

"B? What B?"

"The bee. Hurry up. It's back in the Reading Room. It's starting now."

"Thanks," I mumbled. I had no idea what she was talking about, but I headed to the back of the library. The Reading Room is what they call a function room—they use it for a lot of things that aren't big enough for the Auditorium, like teacher meetings and tests and the blood drive. It has tables and chairs, and a small stage at one end. Nobody ever reads in the Reading Room. The *library* is the reading room, right? What a stupid name.

Along the back wall I could see Mr. Harmon closing the big wooden door that keeps the Reading Room away from the usual riot in the main room. Mr. Harmon, my favorite teacher, looked at me, then he looked at the floor as the door clicked shut between us.

So, of course, I opened it.

The room looked different. The tables were pushed aside. It was pretty crowded. About 60 people were back there. English teachers and several parents were sitting under the big U.S. map. Across from them, under the world map, three rows of kids were twitching in their chairs, looking nervously at green sheets of paper. Whatever was going on, I knew I didn't belong. So I sat down under Florida, next to some parents. Mr. Harmon was sitting behind an enormous dictionary at the front of the room by the stage.

Up came Mrs. Cornell with her turtle head, holding a clipboard and a stopwatch. She shot me a look when I walked in, then she muttered something quiet to Mr. Harmon without taking her eyes off me. He whispered a few words and gave her a "whattya gonna do?" shrug. Finally, she straightened up and stepped behind the podium on the little stage, clearing her super-long throat to speak.

"Parents, students and faculty," she began, "I'm Brigid Cornell, head of the English department. Welcome to the annual schoolwide spelling bee. We should all be proud of these contestants, win or lose, for the effort they've put into studying their word lists. As you know, the winner will represent our school in the citywide bee in two weeks, which will be on local TV. And *that* winner will go to the State finals in January, which will be on cable TV, which is, of course, very exciting. Now, if our students will please put away their word lists, we can . . ."

My hand shot up. "Mrs. Cornell?" I interrupted in my best you're-the-authority voice.

She looked at me over her thin little glasses. She didn't seem to want to answer.

"Yes, Mr. Munn?"

"Mrs. Cornell, I am afraid I forgot to get my little green piece of paper from Mr. Harmon. May I get another?" She shot a look at Mr. Harmon. I looked at Mr. Harmon too, but he was fidgeting with the dictionary.

Mrs. Cornell riffled through the papers tightly stacked on her clipboard, searching for a particular one. "Mr. Munn, you are not on this sign-up sheet. I don't believe . . ."

"Mrs. Cornell, I am afraid I forgot to sign up. Where was the sign-up sheet?"

"In my office. But I'm sorry . . ."

"Mrs. Cornell, was there a cut-off date on your sign-up sheet? I'd really like to sign up for your annual schoolwide spelling bee now."

"I don't think . . ."

"C'mon, sign him up," said somebody's dad from the back row, left-hand side, near Arizona. "What the hell difference does it make if he wants to be in the bee?"

"Let the boy participate," said a mom in mascara and a wig. At least I hoped it was a wig. "For crying out loud."

Mrs. Cornell's mouth looked like it'd just sucked a lemon. She added my name to the list with very loud pen strokes. "Congratulations, Mr. Munn," she said to herself. She said some other things too, but I couldn't hear them. I'm sure they were encouraging.

I shot Mrs. Cornell a peace sign as I shuffled over to the only empty seat, in the last row, under India, next to Juliana Wittenauer. (Notice how perfectly that was spelled.) She immediately pulled her precious little green word list away from my eyes. Welcome to the spelling bee. Time to show off that famous school pride.

Sorry to leave you hanging, Mrs. W. But it's time to go.

See ya.

Thursday, November 4

Okay, Tod. You win. This is a very interesting story. As a former English teacher, I'm happy to say your composition left me hanging. Please continue.

I figured you'd like this story. But please don't call it a composition. That just makes it worse. It's going to take forever to write. I'll try to finish it today, but I'll let you know in advance I'm the only hero.

At this point, I was no longer Tod. I was Speller #31.

Mr. Harmon cleared his throat and sounded a little funny. I couldn't figure out why four other kids from my Honors class were sitting there folding up and putting away those word lists. When did he hand them out? I hadn't missed class in at least a week.

Then I used my best Sherlock Holmes and figured it out. All four of those kids were in Mr. Harmon's Video Club after school. It was the ever-popular Greg Bushwick and the twinkies who follow him around, making lousy short movies and nasty secret ones with the school's video gear. Those mannequins brag and strut around like they're at Hollywood High School. Don't they know how little it means to be a big shot here?

Why did Mr. Harmon leave me out?

Mrs. Cornell was calling the words. The first one, *obeisance*, took two victims. *Chimerical* and *chicanery* also drew blood. *Feasibility* should have been easy, since it sounds just like it's spelled. But two more kids found it unfeasible, including Blind Stuart from my science class.

Everyone seemed to know the exact way to answer, spelling bee–style. First you say the word, then you spell it, then you repeat the word. I couldn't tell if it was an official rule to talk that way, but I wasn't about to get kicked out for answering any differently.

So Mr. Harmon was the guy with the dictionary giving the definitions, and the other English teachers weren't. Did that mean Mr. Harmon was one of the organizers? Was he embarrassed of me? Was he following orders? It's a safe bet

Mrs. Cornell won't be licking envelopes at my fan club anytime soon.

Here are some of the words Mrs. Cornell sent my way: *Misanthropic. Dysfunctional. Indictment. Incarceration.* Clearly she had no idea that I read my own school file.

[Tod, that is a very funny comment.]

Each time it was my turn to answer, more of the original 30 had bitten the dust. After what seemed like forever, there weren't but four of us left.

And then I got a stumper: *excogitate.* I had been proud of the fact that the whole time, I hadn't asked Mr. Harmon to define any of the words I got. But this one got me. I couldn't figure out the vowel after the g. So I asked—you say *define*—and Mrs. Cornell sighed and Mr. Harmon went back to his dictionary. "To excogitate is to reflect deeply on a subject," he said. And I was set. It was just *cogitate* with an ex. So I spelled it correctly, to everybody's chagrin. (Yeah, *chagrin* was another word Cornell thought would stump me, by the way.)

Poignant turned four into three. And somehow I was one of the survivors. Can you believe it? I never was in a situation like this before in my life. I felt like a dweeb on a TV game show.

So there I was in the back row, while Sir Buggery Gushwick, the "director" of Mr. Harmon's video club, was up front. I couldn't see his face, but I could imagine him smiling that fake toothpaste smile like he was practicing for the presidential debates.

Cornell never stopped shooting icicles through her eyes. I still couldn't figure out what was bugging her about me being there, or why she seemed to be giving Mr. Harmon glares and stares too. At least Mr. Harmon seemed to ease up on me when I didn't drop out early. He even asked me a few friendly times to come up to the front row like that stiff Juliana Wittenauer did, but I knew I wouldn't like how it felt up there.

Mostly I just looked at the back of the chair in front of me.

I discovered that I didn't like to look at people whenever I did spelling because it kept me from seeing the words in my head. I couldn't believe how little it took to be a world champion spelling guy. It was just so easy. Usually words sound like how they're spelled, or if they're tricky, then there's something hidden in a word that's a kind of a clue. Every word's got a cousin you've met before, unless it sounds French and it's got all kinds of silent *G*'s and missing *Y*'s, like *poignant*. Then you just have to know them.

Up came *deductible*. Down went Juliana, who thought the *ible* was *able*. Then there was sort of a stunned silence. Did the whole room look uncomfortable or was it just me? Mrs. Cornell stood up and straightened her skirt. She wasn't even holding her clipboard. Instead, she was holding a coffee mug.

"Yes, everyone. Yes. Now we have our two finalists. Congratulations are in order for them already. Gregory Bushwick and Mr. Munn . . . Tod Munn. And in their way they're both winners. Today's runner-up is entitled to a certificate and this mug. And the winner . . ."

Suddenly from the other end of the room came the voice of Mr. Carnegie, our valiant leader and principal, who was holding a handful of junk. "The winner will receive this trophy and this silk ribbon. He will also represent our school with pride at the citywide finals two weeks from Thursday at three p.m. At City Hall. On *television*." He was staring right through me during his entire boring speech, putting tons of emphasis on the final word.

Television. Me. Right. I could feel the heat, or hate. Now I was certain they told Mr. Harmon to keep me out. He's always complimenting my spelling. He knew I would win. They all did. I guess he had to obey; Cornell's his boss. On the one hand, I couldn't blame him. On the other hand, I did.

I could hear the cogs turning in their faulty faculty heads. How did we let this happen? How could it have come down to the Munnster and Greg the beauty queen? This excellent school has an image to keep up. How could we put that horrible animal on television? All they had to do was ask.

Me? In front of a crowd?

Never.

Back to the spelling. Grog and I went back and forth at least a dozen more times. Then he fumbled. He really did. He spelled it *j-e-w-e-l-l-e-r-y* instead of *j-e-w-e-l-r-y* and should have gone down. Carnegie and Cornell looked nauseous. Then they looked at Mr. Harmon, who looked pretty spooked himself. I was getting ready to spell the word correctly when Mrs. Cornell stood up and said, "Wait!" Then she walked over to the jumbo ancient dictionary on the little turning pedestal and spun it away from Mr. Harmon. My principal held up one hand to silence us while the head of my English Department flipped through the brittle thin pages while my teacher simply looked uncomfortable.

"The spelling of *jewellery* is not the common American spelling," she announced, "but it is the common British spelling, and it is included in our dictionary. So the spelling is valid."

At that moment I caught Mr. Harmon looking at me out of the sides of his eyes. My face was all red and hot and my hands held tight to the seat of the chair. I heard that dim ringing sound that makes me lose my temper. I didn't really know why at the time, but I do now.

"Tod?"

Mrs. Cornell was repeating my name and looking a little worried. I must have spaced, because everybody was looking at me, waiting for my next answer. Even Gorgon the Blond shifted around in his throne to see if his favorite low-life volcano might erupt.

"Time's running out, Tod," said Mr. Harmon.

I took a deep breath, and I let it out before speaking.

"L-i-c-e-n-c-e."

Mrs. Cornell shot right up, nearly kicking her chair over. Mr. Harmon got a kind of sorry look in his eye. Unprincipled Carnegie just about clapped his hands.

"Gregory, the word is *license*," said Cornell the Barbarian. And Gregory spelled it the way they wanted.

Back in the main room, Bernie poked his head up from a

Kawasaki ad. "Where were you?" he asked, squinting like he didn't understand his own words. "You didn't do your history paper, did you? You were gonna do mine, too."

"Nah," I said, "I was back with the maps."

Bernie cracked himself up. "Munn, you're so dumb, you're the only guy who gets lost in a map."

"Yeah. Let's go," I said.

Bernie went out ahead through the turnstile. Just after I pushed the cold metal away from me, I stopped at the far end of the checkout desk. Mrs. Lent was standing there, looking at me with her arms folded. I reached in my bag and held out a black coffee mug to her. The mug said "Sit for a Spell." I said nothing as Mrs. Lent took it from my hand and smiled.

Friday, November 5

My head hurts today.

So, I guess if you are expecting another really long notebook entry today, I can't say you're going to get it. My life isn't interesting. It's boring and it's pretty lousy. And this month has been even more boring and lousy than usual. I'm already trying to dig up old stories to entertain you. I don't feel entertaining today. Sue me.

Honestly, I'm getting really tired of my friends carping at me for being here. They give me dirty looks, like I'm some narc who turned them in and got a better deal for my trouble. Well, I didn't. You know that and I know that.

It's pretty much an even swap, the way I see it. They're out in the cold, windy courtyard snagging flyaway homework with pointy sticks, and I'm roasting in this overheated oven. Now I know why this room got painted the color of the desert. At least my droogs get to talk and laugh and goof around after school. I've got to sit here with my mouth taped shut, dumping useless blather in a notebook while you sit at that huge iron desk every day, filling out other people's boring college applications and writing their college essays for them. Rex and Rob are always ragging on me, and even Bernie once complained that I'm in Comfy Town while they do hard time. The way I see it, they get fresh air and exercise while I'm in jail getting writer's cramps.

Honest, Mrs. W., I'm wondering what is really going on. If you think I'm going to break down and spill all kinds of secrets, it's not going to happen, even if you keep your promise and don't show anyone what I write. You won't even tell me what you're looking for. I've never heard of keeping a kid after school to fill up a notebook. Is this some kind of first? This is weird for a guidance counselor to do, right? I mean, where's the guidance? Where's the counseling? Not here. Or maybe you're too smart to try any of that crap on me.

I'm a loser, okay? I was born a loser and I'll live a loser and I'll die a loser. And nothing you do here is going to ever change that. I'm so sick of this crap. I'm done.

Goodbye.

Monday, November 8

Good afternoon, Tod. I know you'll be reading this today, because I had our biggest sentry escort you here from your last class. Before you respond, I want you to think about something. I was extremely unhappy with your attitude Friday, especially your refusal to answer me as you bolted out the door early. Also, the personal work I do in this room after school hours is none of your business. Let's get to the point. Either you complete your daily detention in an orderly manner every afternoon, as agreed, or I will be forced to tell the school's Disciplinary Committee to reopen trespassing, vandalism, and robbery charges against you and your three "friends." If you prefer the latter (and I know you know what that word means), then you're free to leave right now. Just close this journal and you needn't write another word. But if you choose to stay and continue, then I expect you will dedicate yourself to your assignment.

Here's a bit of advice. This most certainly is not jail. As a matter of fact, if I hadn't intervened, you and your friends would be cleaning God-knows-what down at the Juvenile Detention Facility at this very moment. It may help for you to remind your friends that it is <u>you</u> who is keeping their sorry bottoms out of the juvie. That news may not only quiet them down, but prompt them to clean the yard more thoroughly than they have. This is all I intend to say on the matter. Please let me know what you plan to do. —Judith Woodrow

Okay.

Fine.

You win.

Look, I had a really bad headache. I'm not going to give you a violin story, but money's been tight and I had to sell my lunch card and I was late for school so I didn't get anything to eat and I get cranky, really cranky, in the afternoon when I haven't had breakfast or lunch. Okay? Today I had free hot breakfast because you don't need a card for that.

And it's not a journal. It's a notebook.

And I still think it's weird that I'm sitting here without any real instructions except that I should fill a notebook every day with enough pages to cut myself free. How can anybody scrawl his story when he doesn't have anything to say? When he doesn't *do* anything? Why would anyone want to? It's not like life makes any sense. You wake up, you eat, you learn something useful, and you go back to bed. If it's a good day, you take more than you lose. If it's a bad day, try to cut your losses. Make your own rules, and don't break them. Don't let people piss you off, but if they do, make them sorry. And walk away telling yourself that you've still got your pride, even if you've got to fool yourself to keep it. I won't let anybody hurt my pride. Nobody but me.

That's my whole philosophy, okay?

How can I have much of a biography? I haven't even been to jail yet. But if you want more Tales from the Slums, the only story I can think to write here today is about Rex, okay?

So I'll write it down because I'm still trying to figure it out myself.

We were over by the variety store last weekend. Rex and I had just spent some air money on snacks. Little palm-sized chocolate bars and candy with wrappers that don't crinkle in your pocket. That kind of stuff. We were heading to his place for TV, or maybe go to Rob's for video games. It was sunny and cold, a blue-sky fall day. The only clouds I could see were my breath and Rex's smoke.

Rex and I were kicking a rock back and forth across the sidewalk while we walked. Rex is really good at kicking rocks. A couple of times, he chipped a rock off a fire hydrant and it came right back to me. I think Rex could have been a primo athlete if he'd been more serious about practice and cut out the cigs, but he's already a year older than me. He got held back.

A couple of holy rollers were on the corner, holding little booklets for God. There was an old lady and a goober not much older than us, wearing a suit. Rex looked at me with a sideways smile without turning his head my way.

I know Rex. He wanted to jerk them around. Me, I don't have a beef with these people. Even though when they look at me, all they see is a messed-up soul needing major repairs. I know they want to get under the hood, drive me to church next Sunday. They won't ask, but they really want guys like me to reach over and take some booklets, scrub my life clean. Not going to happen. If they were smart they wouldn't waste their paper on me. I carry the stink of a lost cause.

Yeah, when God's People get their eye on me, they think I'm stupid enough to save. They think I'm predictable. Let them. I like it when people figure me out wrong. That gives me some room to work.

So these holy rollers act like they don't want to pin us down, but they do. The young dude looked at Rex and then at me, figuring out which of us was worth his time. Finally, he locked eyes on me and said, "Hello," but very quiet and politely, almost respectfully. Rex jumped right between us. "Push off," he said. The suit stepped back against the brick wall and his face looked peaceful but kind of nervous at the same time. Rex was in a pushing mood. I was not. I ate my chocolate.

"God give you any money, kid? Got any charity for a poor boy like me?" asked Rex with a bit of steel in his voice. Then he burped.

I expected the junior minister to shrink off, but he didn't. He got back his Clark Kent smile and his shoulders eased up. "God helps those who help themselves," the kid said calmly. Hearing this, I was sure he wasn't anywhere older than we are.

"God probably don't like that I helped myself to some beef jerky sticks at that variety store," sneered Rex before he spit on the ground. We were being treated to the full range of Rex's disgusting habits. It was great.

"Every commandment—" started the preacher boy.

"God ain't got nothing over the Devil," says Rex. "The Devil pays in the here and now. Cash on the barrel." That's classic Rex philosophy, which means don't try to figure it out.

During all this, I looked over at the silent old lady companion. She was looking back at us pretty grim through her cheap black fishbowl glasses. I think she was saying *cluck-cluck*, or at least thinking it. She didn't hide her disapproval very well. She wore all black, really sensible stuff, and hanging down from her little round black hat she had one of those veils that widows wear. The kid gave his old lady friend a whisper not to worry, and he took another step forward toward Rex with a gleam that would make a salesman proud.

"Tell me, friend, are you genuinely happy?"

Uh-oh.

"You know what makes me happy? Happy is you goons getting off our sidewalk, leaving folks alone. Fly back to your church, Angel."

"The Lord IS your shepherd," said the boy priest.

"This sidewalk AIN'T your church." Rex spit this last part out through the hole where his bottom front teeth used to be. His jaw was clenched. Two feet away, the kid clearly wanted to get angry back at Rex, but he'd been raised right. His voice was nearly calm. The smile came back.

"The world is our church."

You had to hand it to this kid—he didn't back down easily, and Rex is part caveman. Each of them had his beliefs, but I believe Rex was the only one who had flattened a few dozen bigger and tougher kids. And he didn't have to worry about wrecking his fancy suit, either.

Rex looked around mockingly. "Huh? This world is our church? Well, I'm sorry to say I've been disrespectin' our church my whole damn life."

Rex thought this last zinger was particularly funny, and the kid's big smile got even bigger. Still, I noticed the pastor's hands were both clutching that briefcase pretty tightly. "You'd be singing a different tune, my friend," he said, moving inches from Rex, "if you read your Bible. You'd know all about God's love for every creature."

"God's love?" said Rex, now sounding really puzzled and maybe a little unhinged. "God's LOVE? You friggin' ninny, you know squat about that. You come to this crap-hole street saying God loves us all? God don't love us all."

Rex had put on a face I could not read. He wasn't angry yet, but he wasn't joking either. He looked like he was thinking or something. Then a smallish grin came over his mouth. "You really think God loves everybody?"

"I know it," said the kid.

"I prove you wrong, prove God don't love everybody, and you and your grandma go . . . go away. You two don't come back to this street, deal?"

The street. I had been so sucked into this weirdness that I totally forgot we were on the street, with people and cars going by. I forgot the old lady in her thick black shoes, too. She'd made herself totally invisible. I guess a couple of centuries pushing the Bible in this slum teaches you a few survival skills.

The minister liked Rex's deal. He didn't even look at the

old lady when he answered, all cocky. "We're all God's creatures. He's got work to do on a few of the rougher ones, but no, he loves us all. You'll never be able to prove anything as preposterous as that," he said.

"Right. Sure. We got a deal?" asked Rex, a little impatient. "Don't worry, you don't got to shake hands or nothing."

"Sure, we 'got a deal,'" said the kid, like he had a full house in his hand. "And when you lose, you read this brochure tonight and we talk about it tomorrow. Deal?"

He handed over a brochure instead of a hand, but Rex ignored it. "Yeah. Sure. Deal."

I didn't have a clue what Rex was up to, but if it meant smacking some missionary in front of an old lady, or swiping that briefcase, their friends would empty the pews to get an eye for an eye. This was shaping up to be the kind of trouble I couldn't talk my way out of.

Rex stiffened his back and looked taller. What came next, I still don't believe. Rex belted it out like he was at some church. Then he pointed his finger at the kid, his face all red with hellfire.

"The Lord saw that the wickedness of men was great on the earth, and that all the thought of their heart was bent upon evil at all times!"

People stopped and stared. The kid stuttered. "But th-that's . . ."

Rex wasn't done shouting. "And the LORD said, 'I will destroy man whom I have created from the face of the earth. *For I am grieved that I have made them!*'"

"Lord almighty!" said the old lady. In a flash, she opened her Bible and pointed out a passage to her speechless little friend.

"Damned right," said Rex, sticking out his jawbone and showing off his freaky missing teeth. Then he went on, a bit calmer but now totally threatening. "That Bible's your tree of knowledge? This street's mine. It's my Eden Garden, and I'm the damned snake. You gonna move on?"

This Rex I knew. He was ready for action. But Minister Boy didn't have anything left to say, or if he did, didn't get a chance. The old lady had him by the sleeve of his suit and was tugging him away from us, back toward the variety store. He took a bunch of steps backward, looking at us, trying to think up a comeback before he finally turned around.

Rex called after him, in that loud preacher voice again. "You must not eat from the tree of the knowledge of good and evil, boy, for when you eat of it you will surely die!"

"Praise the Lord," added the old lady. Her boyfriend continued to say nothing, so she gave him his coat sleeve back, and he slumped away.

I stared at Rex. He was grinning like a lottery winner.

"What the hell was that?" I asked, and I meant it.

"Just fightin' fire with fire," said Rex, lighting up half a cigarette. He handed me one of his chocolate bars. I tore it open. It had already started to melt in his hand. "I always hate them guys," he said.

My mouth was full and so was my mind. "Why'd he go?" I spluttered. "What'd you say to him?"

Rex shot me a nasty look and he licked his lips. Then he blew out his smoke all slowly. I knew to stay the hell away and drop things. Rex looks hungry, but he could take a few chucks at me any time with those wiry arms and make them hurt.

We decided to go to Rob's after all. We kicked another rock around and he punted it hard into a passing car's back door. Not even this brought his smile back.

"Don't talk about this with Rob," he finally said. "I was just making up some stuff to clip that dude's wings."

"Sure. No problem," I told him. If I hadn't seen that lady point to her Bible, I would have believed him, too.

Tuesday, November 9

Good afternoon, Tod. I'm glad we're back in business. Your last entry was nicely written. Maybe today you'd like to write about writing?

Well, I don't know about real writing. Or real writers. I don't think writers are like real people. They're different. They know a lot about everything and have a lot to say and people want to listen. They've seen the world. They've all got a house full of books.

I like reading. It's free travel. And I like the writers' quotes on Mr. Harmon's door. He even put a new writer's quote up on the door yesterday. I already memorized it.

It's better to write about things you feel
than about things you know about.
—L. P. Hartley

All of Mr. Harmon's writer quotes are pretty good, but this new one really clicked. I mean, I sure don't know a lot, including who the hell L. P. Hartley is. But writing in this notebook has definitely made me feel stuff. And it's stuff I don't always want to think about.

Like the other day. I had pretty much gotten that whole spelling bee out of the pit in my stomach. A lot of water's gone under that bridge, and I almost went up the river because of it. But I had it under control until I wrote the story down for you. Then stuff started kicking around inside me again.

So I read that new quote just before I walked into Mr. Harmon's room today. It was early, and he was up at his desk, thumbing through a dictionary. That did it—the new quote and the dictionary. While the other kids wandered into the room, I couldn't stop myself asking him what's been bugging me for a whole month.

"Mr. Harmon?"

He put his finger on the word he was looking up, and he looked up.

"Yes, Tod?"

"How come I didn't get one of those little green word lists? For the spelling bee?"

"Well, Tod," he said, laughing, "I suppose you can chalk it up to one of your absences."

"But you never mentioned the bee. Not in class. Never."

He took a quick glance at his dictionary, probably to see if his finger was still on the right word. "I didn't notice. But it was posted on the school web site."

I didn't feel like reminding him that we're not all born with computers. But I was feeling bold enough to say what I did.

"Did Mrs. Cornell tell you to keep the riffraff off your team?"

This stopped him.

"Well, she did . . . um, no, Tod, that's not it. Not it at all. You simply weren't around."

"But I'm the best speller. . . ."

His face turned a little red. A little firm. "Evidently not."

I stared at his finger on the dictionary page for an uncomfortable second. Then I looked back up, into his eyes.

"I wouldn't have spelled *citadel* with an *s*."

Mr. Harmon's eyes shot back to the dictionary. His finger was drifting across the page.

"You and Greg . . ." he began. Then he stopped and started a couple more times. "You and . . . Well, in fairness, Greg said that being on TV made him nervous."

"Right," I muttered, trying not to get angry. "He does his best work *behind* the camera."

Harmon suddenly slammed the dictionary shut with a loud *clump*. Then he looked over the book to the class. "Okay, people. Everyone seated. Right now. Books away. I've got a pop quiz for all of you. Spelling quiz. *Right* now!"

There were groans galore as I shuffled to the back of the room. My face felt red, just like it feels red now. All day long I've been thinking about how Harmon reacted when I mentioned Greg's camera work. It wasn't the reaction I'd been hoping for. But it was what I suspected.

Then, to make things worse, I saw you right after that, putting up the new list of names in the honor roll case. I don't think you saw me.

Why do you do it, Mrs. W? What's the point of announcing the names of our school's non-failures? It's bad luck. Everybody knows what happens to the kids who flame out too soon. They're goners. It's a jinx. These chumps might throw the winning touchdown and be captain of the video club and get mostly A's, but what happens next?

They're sagging on the same barstool for the next 50 years, hustling smokes when they're not pumping gasoline. And they're all wishing they'd been smart enough to lay low in school and have fun instead.

Suckers. There they are, tacked up in a glass case in the main hallway. It's no different than the butterfly exhibit at the science museum downtown. And, just like that moldy case of dead bugs, your list of bookworms never really changes, either.

I really think you shouldn't post the grades ever. It's an invasion of privacy.

Sure, getting good grades is important, but not for the official reasons of glory and power. I've got much smarter reasons than that. You want to know them?

Good grades are like motor oil. They keep out the friction. Teachers don't bug you, and neither do parents. The parents who care, anyway.

Good grades are like insurance. One day they'll save your butt. If you get in trouble or want to check out for a while, they'll buy you some slack time. Earn 'em when you can.

Good grades are a shield. They prove you actually learned something, somehow, and nobody can take that away from you.

Good grades mess with people. They think smart kids get good grades and dumb kids get bad grades. Not true. Any pinhead can memorize facts and pass tests. And some of the smartest kids I know fail because they're bored. Nobody who looks at me thinks I can spell *algebra*, let alone do it. Good. They'll leave me alone.

And most of all, good grades prove that I'm just as smart as the kids who get test preps and tutors. Smarter, maybe, since I don't get test preps and tutors. They can say what they want, but I know it totally bugs them.

Now what about the other kids on the honor roll? Future lawn-care specialists, every one of them.

Life is funny that way.

Hey, thanks again for the sandwich this afternoon, Mrs. W. It's not so easy sitting in the lunchroom without a lunch card.

Wednesday, November 10

Tod, have you ever heard of the study of logic? It's a wise and ancient system for tearing apart false statements. Take your honor roll argument, for instance. On the surface, what you say about grades makes a sort of sense. But scratch the surface and it's nothing but contradictions. You say if you get good grades, you're protected in school. But if you get noticed for good grades, you'll be mowing lawns. That's a new one. And if you get poor grades . . . you're one of the smart kids? Here's what makes sense. I think you don't want your peers to know that you're a smart young man who's on the honor roll every time. Why? What's the downside of intelligence as you see it? I would like to know.

What's the "downside of intelligence"? Are you kidding? In this part of town? Brains make you nothing but a target. A lonely target. And if you're any bit smart and you don't have money, what's left for you? Not college. Not a suit job. Not a big house. Just reminders all day long that you're a small cog in the big machine.

In my neighborhood, you can either be the hard-working nobody or the high-flying somebody. The good guys get ground to a pulp. The bad guys get remembered. What other choice is there for a guy like me?

Anyway, having good grades doesn't mean anything at home. They don't earn me homemade cookies. They don't get me hugs or gold stars or keep me warm, either. Remember the ice storm Sunday? It was too cold to stay in my so-called room. The furnace had died a few days before. And the wind was whistling a never-ending tune on my six-dozen murky glass windowpanes.

It's not a bedroom. It's a porch. A Porsche. A convertible Porsche. It's small, it's uncomfortable, it's useless in the winter, and the top is stuck in the open position.

So I was forced to sit in the front room and watch TV in my coat with my hands buried in my pockets. But the worst part was Sunday-morning TV, cable-free misery, strictly for the elderly. Mom and Dick were parked in the back room, as usual, basking in the heat of the stove.

I don't think I told you about my house before. Here's the grand tour. It's a rectangle. You walk in the front door, my room is an immediate left turn. Behind my room is Mom's room. That's the west wing. The east wing is the front room, which is really just a wide hallway leading to the back room of our runty shack. There's a TV on one wall and a gold velvety couch on the other, which you walk between all day long. There's also a skinny stick lamp, but it needs a new lightbulb.

Our TV used to be against Mom's bedroom wall until Dick moved in. Then it was too loud no matter what I was watching or how quiet the sound was. I hate golf, but once I turned it on low just to see if Dick would complain. He did.

I never go into Mom's room since Dad left, but there's only one place for a bed—in the corner against the living room wall (where their pillows go) and against my bedroom wall (the side Dick sleeps on). Lucky me, the only two places I sit are on my bed or on the couch, six plywood inches from the sleeping Dick. Moving the TV to the other wall has helped keep the peace, except for the times I knock their wall with my elbow. Then look out.

The only thing that separates the front room from the back room is an archway that's nearly as wide as the house. Just before Lincoln was president, there were sliding doors that could separate these spaces. They're long gone. Pass under the archway and you're in the back room. It's not a kitchen, not really. It's more like a dining room with the world's first stove and sink. Someone had a gas jet installed eons ago in that huge iron stove, but that baby can still burn wood (or whatever you've got) when you have futility paying the utilities.

This place was built around the Civil War; I'm not kidding. And the guy who built it didn't spend a lot. In those days, kitchens didn't have all kinds of built-in appliances and cupboards hanging off the wall. You stuck a wood stove in the corner, made a big plank table, and put everything on shelves. Closets and cabinets were pieces of furniture you had to buy. That's why there aren't any closets in the whole house. None. Everything I've got to wear is in a dresser or on a chair. Or on my back. I keep my important stuff in a suitcase under my bed. I've never gone anywhere where I'd bring a suitcase. That's something I'd like to do one day. Get on a bus or something and use a suitcase.

Anyway, Dick was cooking up some eggs that he had, and Mom was mending something big and orange in her sewing corner, which looks out the back window. She was cranking the old pedal sewing machine with her foot. Treadle, she calls it. It's a seesaw for your foot that makes the needle go up and down. That old Singer machine is our antique, our treasure. It's the golden goose around here. Well, not golden. Maybe tin.

It would have looked like a real cozy family scene, if I knew what one looked like. Dick isn't what anyone would call a cook, so I think his sudden burst of gourmet activity had more to do with hogging the heat from the stove than the sudden joy of feeding his loved ones. Plus I don't think Mom said a single sentence to him all weekend that didn't have the word "furnace" in it. Dick reminded her about forty times that furnace repair guys don't come on Sundays. Mom pointed out that they do come on Saturdays and Fridays, the day the furnace crapped out. Dick replied that furnace guys like to be paid for their work. Mom said that's what credit's for. Dick laughed his head off and flipped the frying pan over onto a plate.

"You got any more eggs?" I called, sitting on my hands to keep them warm.

"You see a waiter, he'll take your order," Dick said, laughing, as he dumped half a bottle of hot sauce on the scrambled eggs. I don't mind hot sauce, but not on eggs. On chicken wings. That's good.

Dick moved over to the square table and sat down. I got up and headed back to get something to eat. Mom and Dick and the table were on the left, behind their bedroom. Sewing corner behind the table. Stove and sink on the right. Back door on the back wall. That's it. Just before the backyard is a tiny porch. That's where the fridge is. They keep it unplugged and open all winter to save on the electric bill. In the summer we move it back in. With this brilliant system, the fridge is always in the most uncomfortable place to be. I'm sure I'm the only kid I know who zips up his winter coat to get a glass of milk.

"There's no more eggs," I said. In fact, there was no more anything but butter and a couple of pounds of hamburger in a plastic bag.

Mom gave Dick a look and went back to her sewing. She had an orange thread in her mouth that she needed to break, but it wouldn't snap. Her hands were full of that orange thing—a blanket or curtains, maybe—and she was holding a stitch in place with her hands. Mom looked at me with her mouth full of thread. I picked up her scissors, leaned over, and cut the thread close by the stitching. I would have just bit it in half.

Mom spit out the thread and spoke to me in her nice voice. "Go into my room and get the space heater. Keep it in your room until he gets the furnace back up."

Dick swiveled around. "That's my heater," he said.

Mom didn't answer. She sent a reply with her round, round eyeballs. Both Dick and I heard her loud and clear: *It's my house. It's my house. It's my house.*

And Dick swiveled right back around to his spicy eggs.

I was glad my mom offered the space heater, but it smells

really bad, like hair burning. The thing was ancient. After I carried it to my room, I looked on the back and found a little metal plate. *Finn Portable Fire. Buffalo 7, New York*.

Buffalo 7? This thing was *so* ancient, it was made before zip codes. And speaking of codes, I'm sure it didn't live up to the fire codes, either.

"The hamburger is for dinner, Tod. There's some money in the jar. Go get some bread and peanut butter at Colson's."

As I hope you never discover, Mrs. W., Colson's is the skinny little local deli that used to be somebody's living room. It's always dark and it stinks like cat piss.

I dumped the coins from the jar into my pocket. "Can I get some eggs, too?"

"There isn't enough, I don't think. Get the sandwich stuff. Anything else you can get, be my guest."

"When's the hamburgers?" I called from the doorway.

"Six, six thirty. You don't have to come right by. I'll save you one," she said quietly.

Good. I grabbed my history book and headed off to Bernie's.

So, that's my home, okay? The furnace works now, but you'd never know it. I'm a lucky guy. I get to go from the world's least-heated house to the world's most-heated school. It's amazing I haven't caught ~~pnu pnue~~ ~~pnumo~~ pneumonia yet.

[Tod, do you realize this was the first time you've asked me to spell a word?]

[Tell that to Mrs. Cornell, okay?]

It's so baking hot in this building every winter. Today in school, while I was on my way to start the card game at lunch, I thought I smelled something suspicious, like fresh air. I wondered if a cold draft might be sneaking around the corner from the main entrance where the statue is. Something bad might happen to the sphinx if the temperature ever dipped below 100. He's used to the desert, right? So I went out of my way just because you've got me doing good deeds nowadays.

Turns out the front doors were closed. I opened them a crack and I shut them again, stopping the draft before it started. The guard didn't even look up from her newspaper to thank me. Since I was already standing there, I figured I might as well take another quick glance at the sphinx-mobile. It was made of clay and probably baked in a kiln. She painted it really well. It's hard to paint for a kiln because you have to use a different color than the one you want. The oven changes the colors a lot. Brown becomes light blue, or light blue becomes brown, I don't remember. Either way, when I tried it in fourth grade, I got it wrong.

The paint on the sides of the tires looked real. I mean, they looked like real tires. The sphinx had a smile that was pretty much like the real sphinx's, but this guy seemed to be having fun in his convertible anyway. I looked very closely at the wheels. Even the hubcaps on the wheels were the right color. They were silver.

"What do you think?" asked a girl's voice behind me. Luz. She was lugging her big leather art briefcase and wearing a smock. "It's a work in progress. Give me a hand, huh?"

Luz handed me a tiny pair of black plastic sunglasses. "I got 'em from Mr. Potato Head," she admitted. "You're tall. Can you get 'em on Mr. Chops without busting his head off?"

"I don't know. Sure. Probably."

"Don't sound so confident," she said, but at least she was smiling. "Here."

"How come you're messing with this?" I asked her, reaching my arm delicately up over the statue. Delicately for me, at least. "Wasn't it good enough to be the Sculpture of the Year?"

"God, no. At this school? Talk about an empty honor. Who's Phister going to get next month? Anyway, he's such a perv. Move them down a little so he's peeking over the tops, will you?"

"I could if he had a nose."

"How's he going to have a nose? Didn't Napoleon's army shoot it off in, like, 1800?"

"You're asking *me*?"

"Look, the glasses have gotta go a little lower. Hold on." She reached in her mouth and took out her chaw of gum. Green lifeless gum. Each of her fingernails was painted a different color. She handed the gum to me like it was a gold coin.

"Here, take this."

"You're kidding, right?"

"Stick it on the glasses and put 'em on right. Nice and low. Jack Nicholson. Yo! Perfect the first time. Good going, Ace."

I walked back to the lunchroom. I didn't know if there was any time left to eat, or what time it was. The card game was on, but I didn't care. Rex was in my seat. Dandruff Derek was playing across from him with his back to me. I couldn't see his face, but man, I could tell. Bernie waved. I nodded and looked around the lunchroom. Suddenly, the whole room looked strange. So I went up to the library instead.

Thanks for the sandwich again today. I liked the tuna one better.

Thursday, November 11

Tod, I've just found out that I won't be here tomorrow, so you have a reprieve. There's no detention tomorrow. Enjoy the afternoon. And please hold on to your lunch card next week. —JW

Ms. Woodrow, I'm not sure what I could say to cheer you up. I really appreciate all the sandwiches this week. I can already see you're having a bummer day just by the way you're staring out the window and sighing. Not that you're going to tell some teenager your problems. But whenever something happens and it isn't fair—which happens to me A LOT—I toss rocks into a trash basket. Seriously. Take a bunch of small rocks and sit back a ways from your trash can. Start aiming them into the can. They make a lot of noise when they go in. Pretty soon, after a couple dozen rocks, all that matters is aiming and making noise. Collect 'em up and throw 'em again. Pretty soon you're in a groove, throwing 15, 20 in a row without missing any. You're feeling pretty good. You're making a racket. And you've killed maybe a half hour. That's a half hour you forgot how much life sucks.

You probably won't want to do that in school, though. Save it for home.

Okay, here's something else. I wasn't planning to write about it, but you wanted happy stuff, so here goes. I went to my locker at the end of the day and there was a piece of electric pink paper sticking through the air slots. It was all folded up into a little rectangle. I figured it was a guy who folded it because it would take some serious hand strength to get it that small. Seeing that it was a pink paper, I was ready for another stupid prank from somebody pretending a girl was writing me a love note. I get those. These geeks think it crushes me to be reminded I'm not someone's secret crush.

But it wasn't a note, not a handwritten one. It was one of those audition flyers for the new school play. You know the one, it's up on every wall.

IT'S CALLED A PLAY
BUT IT'S GOING TO BE WORK

I snorted a laugh. Whoever wrote that really knows how to motivate people. It might as well have said *Scrub Floors! Empty*

Trash! Hate Every Minute! I thought about who might have pulled this stunt. It could have been anyone. My handful of friends. My schoolful of enemies. The list of suspects was as long as the yearbook, and just as boring. I unfolded the neatly creased paper one more time, then crumpled it properly and aimed it at the nearest trash can. Like a rock.

Just as the wad was leaving my hand, something bumped me. I rolled into the locker doors. The paper skidded down the hall. Textbooks fell at my feet. My brain started gathering information.

Jeremy Gibson. Kneeling. Apologizing. Quickly picking his books off my sneakers. Two giraffes from the tennis team hustled down the hall, laughing in their sweaters.

"Oh, man, Munn, I'm sorry. Pete and Foster shoved me. Really . . ."

This could work to my advantage. My foot pressed his math book to the floor. "Gibson. That's going to cost you a dollar."

Gibson stood up with the rest of the books in his hands. "Oh, man, Munn. I didn't mean it. Those guys—"

"They're gone. You're here. And I'm not happy. I want a dollar."

"I don't have one. I already gave my . . ." And then his face went white as his voice went silent. Gibson was scared he'd leaked something. But what?

I put my hand rather firmly on his shoulder. Things were starting to make sense. "Who?" I demanded. Who else was borrowing money from my wimpy rich kids?

Gibson spit out one letter. "I . . . I . . ." and then he turned and fled, leaving his math book under my foot. He was definitely spooked.

[Tod, how exactly was this story supposed to be cheering me up?]

I bent down to pick up the book when I saw two large eyeballs staring up at me. Not real ones, but crazy Egyptian eyes—one on each toe of a hand-painted sneaker.

"Hi, Luz."

Holding the book and standing up straight, I looked into her mascara-raccoon eyes. She didn't say anything but she had my back against the locker. It looked like she was daring me to move. She wasn't going to kiss me, was she? Then she cracked her gum and handed me a familiar pink piece of paper, all creased and folded again.

"You gonna do this or what?"

"What? That was from you?"

"Who else would it be from? Alfred Hitchcock?"

"Who?"

"Get off it, Mister Munn. I need your help. Show up at 3:00 tomorrow, back of the auditorium. Okay? The Jeremy Gibsons of the world will thank you."

She walked off, and I tossed the flyer into my locker. *Slam!*

"So, you like that girl, huh?"

I jumped out of my skin. Blind Stuart from science class had snuck up behind me.

"What are you talking about, Stu?"

"That girl. Your voice changed when you were talking to her."

"No it didn't," I said. Because it didn't.

"Okay. See you later, Tod."

He always says that.

"No you won't, Stu."

I always say that back.

Off he went, not even using a cane. He counts footsteps. I stared hard at my locker door.

Me in a play. That makeup has gone to her brain.

I'm not going to her audition. Guaranteed.

Friday, November 12

I went to her audition.

I didn't want anything to do with her play. Or with her. I still don't. I only went to see who would be dumb enough to audition.

It's not even a real play that people have heard of. It's written by a kid. Besides, she's an artist, not a writer. And the rest of those Drama Club kids are weird. They've all got an act, they're all faking who they are. And forget about their clothes—they look like what my mom can't mend.

Everything about a school play is too hokey for words. It's worse than joining chorus or chess club even. Remember last year when they did that Rainbow play? My English teacher made us sit through twenty whole minutes and that was like surgery. I couldn't believe how bad the acting was. I was praying to fall asleep.

What else do you expect from a low-performing school? Oscar winners? I will admit I enjoyed the time they did parts of *West Side Story* and Freddy Robman brought the real knife to the rumble and Terry Ludd ran off the stage. That made it more realistic. But people like me are allergic to happy events. That stuff is for kids whose families buy tickets and applaud. I come from a long line of tomato throwers.

Sure, okay, I thought about Luz and her stupid play today. But here's what I thought . . .

Me in a play? I wouldn't do it. Not in a million years. Too bad the flyer said one of the characters is a criminal. Somebody with flair could pull it off. Somebody with life experience. I understand what makes these guys tick. I'd be a natural. Maybe I wouldn't have to act. I could be myself and that'd put fear into the audience.

I decided I wouldn't do the play even if she asked, but I'd be happy to hear her ask me to be the criminal in her play. Then I'd say no.

Anyway, there could be something to see backstage. I almost never go down that back hallway, except to go to the nurse's office every now and then. I thought about taking Bernie with me, give me someone to laugh with, but he had probably gone to the yard shed to get his rake. Maybe there'd be something I could use back there, something just lying around that nobody seemed to want anymore. That's why I didn't want Rob or Rex with me. I didn't need the competition. I was sitting on the bench outside the nurse's office—you know, building up my energy, getting ready to go around the corner to the backstage door.

Then I heard the scream.

It was a loud girl-scream, like in a horror film. It came rolling around the corner like a windstorm. There was so much scream I couldn't figure out what was going on. Maybe the screamer saw a rat in the hall. Maybe it was puke, or blood. Maybe a light fixture fell on her head. Whoever it was, she knew how to get your attention.

Another girl brushed past me and headed straight into the mystery. I didn't see who it was, I only smelled her. She smelled nice. Another scream followed her. Now I had to look.

I've heard 30 fifth graders having their first recorder lesson. I've heard a flock of gulls fighting over the rotted meat in a supermarket dumpster. I've even heard the long metal moan of an overhead garage door being torn from its tracks by a bread truck. But none of these sounds can compare to the screech of girls when they first see each other after school.

It wasn't a murder scene. Three cute, well-dressed girls were looking at a phone. I knew them all. Karen and Madison and Marla, the lead singers of the Most Popular Girl chorus. They've been a gang since the invention of alphabetical seating.

Marla was holding up the phone, which had some guy's

picture in the screen. It worked like a magnet, pulling the three of them together in a circle. They shouldered around each other, a football huddle of wannabe cheerleaders closing off their privileged circle with a *click*.

"Look at this one with the surfboard?" said Marla with her curly, curly hair.

Madison bit her glossy red nails. "He's too cute in those shorts!" she groaned.

"I want to *own* him," said Curvy Karen.

While Marla thumbed through the phone photos, they screamed some more. Then the conversation turned to the audition.

"I don't know anything about the play?" said short, bouncy Marla, who always sounds like she is asking directions.

"Yeah, except Luz Loser seems to be in charge. Like, where's the teachers?" said long-haired, brown-eyed Karen.

"She gets her hands in everything?" complained freckled, fluffy, fake-eyelash Marla.

"Everything except boys," sneered boyfriend-with-a-car Madison.

"Oh, she can get boys if it's dark enough," said perfect-skin Karen, laughing. "Then she *sucks their blood*!"

Huge laughs here.

"So, we're really going to audition?" asked puffy-lipped Marla.

"We're going to audition and take this play over," decided leader-of-the-pack Karen. "Who cares what it's about? It's the only play we've got. Luz Loser posted three women's parts. We're three women. She desperately needs charisma. We're the best star power this place has. It's as simple as that."

Not surprisingly, her friends agreed.

I waited for the three of them to vanish through the stage door. I'll admit I followed Karen's perfume all the way in. After all, I'm a guy.

Once I stepped inside, I wondered whether or not to tell Luz about the nasty things Karen's Klub was saying about her in the hallway. I decided against it. That's against my rules.

I leaned against the auditorium door, not going in but not leaving, either. In addition to the crowd outside in the hallway, the backstage area was buzzing with a couple dozen kids. I had no idea there were this many dweebs interested in public humiliation. Many of the kids were still holding their hot pink fliers. I had long-since shoved mine into my pocket, where I was crumpling it with my left hand.

"Move it, Munn. Humans coming through." Even in an artsy place like this, I don't get the respect I deserve.

I slouched away from the doorway and found myself backstage. It was an interesting place with the smell of a workshop. A collection of fat ropes ran behind the curtains and along the wall, probably for raising and lowering sets. The ropes led up into the rafters. A catwalk ran across the ceiling. That's where James Bond would be, spying on his mortal enemy, Blofeld. Back on the ground, a huge old sound and light board was close to the stage opening. It was covered with black metal dials, long sliding levers, and antique toggle switches, like the world's first stereo. The high stool behind the console was made of wood and bolted to the floor. A hundred names of people and plays had been carved on it. As I looked around, I saw the names of people and plays and years scribbled on every wall, on the floor, even across the back of the curtains. I guess if an actor really wants to be remembered, it has to be for his signature.

A metal pipe clanged and clattered to the floor. Everyone jumped. Someone backstage yelled, "Sorry!"

"Watch it!" yelled Luz, in no particular direction. "I gave my word nobody would get killed back here."

Luz was standing in the middle of the stage, surrounded by a sudden band of admirers. She was holding a clipboard jammed with a rainbow assortment of papers—bright purple, neon blue, hot pink, and so on. This was really funny, because Luz wasn't wearing a single color. Just black and white and mostly black. She even had a heart-shaped black teardrop drawn under her eye to complete the "don't date me" picture.

A blinding yellow sheet of paper drifted from Luz's clipboard to the floor. By the time she noticed it, someone was already handing it back to her.

"Here you go, Luz!"

It was Karen. Can you believe it?

Luz put the clipboard in her armpit and whistled with four fingers. People covered their ears. "Okay, people. Actors pay attention. Girls line up stage left. Boys stage right. No! No! Stage right is your right when you're looking at the audience. Okay?"

I don't know why my legs started moving at that moment, but they were determined to bring me to the right side of the stage.

"Tod! Munn! C'mere."

Luz said *c'mere* but she was actually walking to me. I could tell that look in her eye. Luz wanted to hand me a part, didn't need me to audition, didn't want me to embarrass the other kids. The fix was in, and she was sparing their feelings. Kind of decent of her.

Her voice was quiet, conspiratorial. Felt a little weird and special all at the same time.

"Look, thanks for coming. I was hoping you would. Means a lot. You can really make this thing work out. I'm depending on you, okay?"

"Okay."

"Thanks, I knew I could count on you. Tonight will you ask your mom if she'd mind sewing the costumes? I'll get her a list. Okay? Cool." Then she clapped her hands a few times and was off to the kids in the lineup.

I stood there for a while and didn't say anything, didn't think anything or feel anything. I just stood there like a tree. Then I resumed my slouch, put down my head, and walked straight between both lines of kids—straight down the short flight of stairs to the first row of seats. Straight into the audience.

I strolled slowly up the aisle, from row A to row Z and through the double letters, all the way to row LL. The Last of the Last. The Loser's Lounge. That's what I call it. That's the only row my droogs and I approve. There's nobody behind us. Nobody but a wall.

Just before I opened the door at the top of the aisle, I turned around, hands in my pockets, my chin on my chest. I raised my eyes from the sea of seats to the wannabe actors lined up so nice on the stage. Luz was pointing to the ceiling and giving some kind of instructions. The lights were almost as bright in the last row as they were on the stage. My neck craned. I blocked the light with my hand. It could have been mistaken for a salute, a farewell to this stupid play of hers. I couldn't wait to get out of there. My shoulders slouched forward as I leaned backward into the door's bar. This was all a stupid mistake.

The weight of my butt opened the door.

"Pops!"

Rex and Rob had been standing against the other side of the same door. Not what I needed.

"We thought that was you," said Rob, loud and laughing. "I told Rex you'd gone to audition for the play. That so? You gonna be an actor?"

I gave Rob a shove. "Are you kidding? Break the sacred Rebel Code of Honor? How dare you accuse me of . . . of . . . of . . . conforming."

Rob grinned his expensive, shiny, orthodontic grin. "You gonna be an actor! Another Bill Shakespeare!"

"Last I heard, Rob, Shakespeare was the writer, not the actor."

"Whatever. Your girlfriend's going to have you hopping around in green tights," said Rob, giggling like a twit.

"Drop it," said Rex, shooting Rob a look that stopped his laughter fast. "Pops here is just getting some inside info. I know him. He's figuring out a way to cause a little trouble. Got a plan?"

"Nothing new. Aren't you garbage men supposed to be outside farming candy wrappers about now?"

Rex hesitated a second and looked around. "Janitor told us to wait here while he gets the lock clippers."

"I'd love to borrow those," said Rob.

"Why the clippers?" I asked.

Rex let out a cigarette-smelling burp and smiled a gappy smile. "Someone put glue in the lock to the tool shed. Jammed it up. Can't get the rakes and bags."

The janitor appeared around the corner, holding the long lock clippers that usually announce the grand opening of a budding criminal's locker. Walking briskly next to him was George, one of the sentries, jabbering into his walkie-talkie. "Yeah, they're here," he said to someone. They moved closer. The color drained out of Rob's face, while Rex's face just hardened.

I leaned close and whispered. "You're a genius, Rob. Absolute genius. Everyone wants to gum up the shed lock. Nobody's going to suspect you," I said. "Write me from jail."

George the sentry, the one who used to be a wrestler on TV, put his hand on Rob's elbow. Knew better than to touch Rex. As they rounded the corner, Rob turned and waved. "Give her a kiss for me," he shouted.

"Who?" I yelled back.

"Luz. Woodrow. Doesn't matter. All your women own you, actor boy!"

"Better than being a stray!" was all I could think of. I hope he heard me. I leaned over and opened up the auditorium door. Luz was singing. Then I slammed it shut again. Stupid Rex. Stupid Rob. Stupid Bernie if he were here. Stupid Luz. Stupid school play. Stupid school. Stupid, stupid, stupid.

Stupid me.

I can't believe I even let myself think such stupid thoughts. I can't believe I thought for five seconds I wanted to be in that stupid mascara raccoon's stupid play. Stupid audition. Stupid costumes. Stupid sneakers don't make enough noise when you kick the floor. Stupid guard not even at her desk. Stupid metal detector. Stupid sphinx in a stupid car. Stupid pedestal bumping my stupid shoulder. Stupid front door. *Slam. Crash.*

Three steps past the front door I froze like a statue. A broken plaster statue. I didn't dare turn around. I squinched my eyes tight, fighting the sunlight. I leaned against the brick wall just left of the doors, head down low.

"No," I told myself. "That didn't just happen." I put my arms around my stomach, trying to breathe better. I launched a desperate wish into the air. "Let's go back ten seconds. Back to the empty guard station, the metal detector." Like every wish, it fizzled and crashed. Crashed like the sphinx.

Now I understand our bond, I thought. I know what we have in common. The statue and I are both alike. We're both lying busted on different sides of the same door.

I exhaled like I'd just been hit by Thor's hammer. But common sense returned. My eyes flicked left, right, ahead. There was nobody around, nobody coming through the front door. I put my hands against the cold bricks and pushed myself back up to a standing position. Nobody had seen me. Under the protection of my wall I knelt down, pretending to tie my sneaker. My eyes wouldn't follow my orders. They traveled across the ground, through the wire-mesh glass, inside the door. I didn't want to see anything. What I did see was enough—a broken silver hubcap, a steering wheel, a spray of small plaster chunks. And a pair of tiny black plastic sunglasses. Upside down.

Voices coming. Time to go. Feeling stupid and getting caught are entirely different things. I had to think. I adjusted my shoulder bag, hiked up my pants, and walked around the corner. A city bus was just pulling into the bus stop. The driver honked at a car blocking its way. At least I had a plan. I had to hustle. I jogged a bit, turned right, and reached for the side door. It was stuck, but a little force got it open. I ran up the stairs and found my usual seat. Up in detention.

Outside, on the street, the bus was still honking.

I know I wasn't supposed to come up to detention today. You already said you wouldn't be here. There's only me, a castaway in the sea of desks. But I needed to write this all down. You still have my notebook, so I'm using a different one, with yellow paper. I'll just staple the pages in later.

I'm so sorry. I'm just so sorry. I didn't mean to hit the pedestal. I didn't even see it. I was just mad at Luz and Rex and Rob and my mom and everybody. Now the statue is busted. The only thing in this ugly school worth looking at. Please don't tell on me, Mrs. W. I wish it never happened. I wish that stupid statue never broke. I wish I could make it up to Luz. But you know how crappy wishes are. You know how crappy everything is. You promised I wouldn't get in trouble for what I wrote. I don't want to get in trouble for this. Not when I feel so bad already.

That's why I came home to finish this super-long notebook entry. I've been writing all evening. It's bedtime already.

I can't believe what I did to the Artist of the Month. I can't wish it and I can't fix it and I can't pay Luz what it's worth. If I could make this stupid thing go away, I'd even get my mom to make those stupid costumes.

Wherever you had to go on such short notice, Mrs. W., I hope your day wasn't as lousy as mine.

Monday, November 15

Bernie didn't come by again this morning, so I got some extra sleep. It sucks that he's got to have a sick mom in the hospital just to let me sleep in, but something's got to be the silver lining, right?

There aren't any other silver linings out there. I had a lousy dream about falling off the big federal building downtown. You don't have to be a shrink to know what I was dreaming about. If I'd dreamed about being Michelangelo maybe I could have carved a new statue to replace that other one.

My mom was already at her sewing machine when I went into the kitchen before school. Her foot was working up and down steadily as she passed a black jacket under the wheel. I stood behind her, thinking about costumes and statues and goth girls and not a single word came out of me. I just hovered, with my heart pounding double-time.

"If you're thinking about mugging people, you'll need practice. I can hear your breathing a mile away."

"No, I'm . . ."

"Guy pays five, six hundred dollars for a sport coat. Cashmere. Tears a hole in it and dumps it at the cheapest dry cleaner he can find. Now it's my problem."

"I . . ."

She turned around, suspicious.

"What *do* you want? Don't they give you a hot breakfast at school?"

". . ."

I dreaded every bit of today and it hadn't even started yet.

"Never mind."

"Good. I've got a mountain of clothes over here and more at the cleaners. I'm buried alive. Today after you get sprung from detention, I need you to pick up another bundle of dirty, ripped clothes so I can sew them and feed you. Got that?"

"Yeah."

"Mrs. Tagliapietra is going to give you an envelope, too. The money's all counted. You dig?"

My mom says prehistoric things like "You dig?" and "Are we cool?" and to tell you the truth, it's embarrassing.

"I dig."

I answer her back the same way, to get her to stop. It hasn't worked yet.

"Cool. Now don't be late."

On the bus I saw Rashawn Cummings sitting in the back with his headphones on. He tried to ignore me, but I knew he was watching out of the corner of his eye. I moved over closer and he opened his book quickly to start reading.

I pulled away one side of his headphones so he could hear me. "What're you reading, Rashawn?"

He gulped. "A book."

"How is it?" I asked, sounding very interested.

"Good."

"Mind if I look?" I let the headphones snap back on his ear and picked the book out of his hand. *Beginning Principles of Algebra*.

"Sounds like a fun read. In fact . . ."

He interrupted suddenly. "Tod, I'm really sorry, I don't have anything to lend you anymore!"

"Any . . . *more*? You mean, like, forever? I don't even know what to say, Rashawn."

He squirmed like a snake and squeaked like its meal. "I mean today. Just today. Nothing today."

There wasn't anything I could do on the bus. That was neutral territory, not worth the penalty. But I knew I had to do something. Had to say something.

"I'm not very smart, Rashawn, so you'll have to explain later. See you on the other side of the metal detector."

Over my shoulder I could hear laughing. Karen Dominick and her friends were nodding and having a good chuckle. At my expense. I just know it.

Luz and her costumes. Mom and her bag of mending. Bernie's mom and her hospital. Rex and Rob. Rashawn and his empty pockets. The statue. As I approached the front door of the school, I tensed myself. I was ready for another sock in the stomach from the empty pedestal, the pile of dust, and the stupid comments from everybody. I didn't think anything else could go wrong.

But something *was* wrong. The smiling face of the sphinx beamed down at me from up high. The statue was back on the pedestal. Unbroken. Absolutely, impossibly unbroken. Exactly as it shouldn't be. Wishes aren't supposed to work that way.

Criminals always get caught going back to the scene of the crime. They can't get enough of the thrill, I guess. Me, I don't get any excitement making trouble, and I sure don't get any relief getting caught. The line at the metal detector was too short to let me take a good look as I passed by the statue. I got so distracted that Rashawn was able to duck away after his bookbag search. I knew I couldn't really examine the statue until lunchtime. But how could I think about anything else all morning? Fortunately, we had a video in science class, so I didn't have to worry about the teacher interrupting me. And Stuart wasn't there, so I didn't have to explain an action-packed video about eggs.

Evidence. I needed evidence. What was the evidence? I know I heard the crash. I saw the broken pieces spread out by the door. Glue? There was too much damage, too much plaster. Not enough time. Luz had probably stayed in the auditorium until pretty late, ordering people around. If she hadn't been so bossy this wouldn't have happened.

Math crawled by on turtle legs. Nothing was making sense. Was this something bigger? It was feeling huge. Not like a miracle or anything hokey like that. I'm thinking it was a rift in the time-space continuum. Something major like that was definitely happening. Especially if the statue hadn't been glued. When the bell rang I handed in my math paper without even crumpling it. I took the stairs two at a time, then rounded the corner.

"Slow down!" yelled George the washed-up wrestler sentry, pointing his walkie-talkie antenna at me. I slowed down, but not until I passed the lunchroom and was nearly at the metal detector. I headed toward the front door and stopped at the pedestal to pretend to fumble in my bag. I peeked up.

No chips. No cracks. No peeled paint. No globs of glue. This wasn't a sphinx. It was a phoenix, back from the dead. I mean, they're almost spelled the same.

I hate to admit it, Mrs. W., but I had all the evidence I needed. There was no denying the cold, hard facts. My sad little wish had come true. Nothing else could explain the impossible rewind of time. Now I'll have to live up to my end of the bargain. If I want to avoid the firestorms and lightning bolts that come with breaking my word, I'm going to have to get those costumes made for Luz. And my mom sure isn't going to be any help.

A promise is a promise. I wish I hadn't written down my wish. Now I can't pretend it never happened.

Only one question. What the hell am I going to do?

Tuesday, November 16

I guess the first thing to do was figure out the first thing to do. That didn't take long. All I had to do was to stand in the lunch line.

"Did ya talk to your mom yet?"

Luz's voice came from out of nowhere.

"Jeez, you nearly gave me a heart attack."

"That's okay. Did she say she'll do the costumes?"

"What's okay, a heart attack?"

"I've got the list here. Let's sit down and go over it."

"Sorry, I've got a card game. If you want, we can talk in Art class."

"Forget it," she said. "I do art in Art. I do business in Lunch."

Suddenly I was aware of a very anxious feeling, and it didn't have anything to do with her dreaded costumes. We had been moving along the lunch line and it was about time to pay. There was no way—NO way—I was going to pull out my new free lunch card with Luz so close. I started fumbling around in my pockets for money that I knew wasn't there. Stupid Rashawn.

Luz chirped up like a way-too-loud bird. "Lost your card? You can use mine. I've got a few extra punches on it."

One of my eyebrows poked up, threatening to cause a smile. I fought it. "You get free lunch?"

"You kidding? You think we'd live near this school if we could afford to move?"

Luz leaned over me and my tray, handing her card to Nardine, the lunch lady. "You can punch it twice."

Nardine made a sarcastic cooing sound. "Ain't that sweet?"

As we headed back to the tables, I tried to break away for the card game. Luz wasn't letting go that easily. She seems to get what she wants.

"Let's sit over there by the windows," she said.

"Let's talk after school."

"Give me your phone number and I'll call your mom."

"Let's sit by the windows," I said.

I waited for her to sit and then I sat across from her, because boyfriends sit next to their girlfriends at lunch. She took the seat with her back to the window, which meant she got to look out on the room. That should have been my seat, but I wanted the fewest number of people to see us talking together. Fortunately, she spoke at the same machine-gun speed used by TV announcers to hide how they trick you.

"Okay, here's the list. I've done a really thorough job. I'll talk slow so you can follow along."

"Thanks."

"We've got seven characters. Seven actors. Like I told you,

it's 1899. It's immigrants. Huddled masses. Straight off the boat. Lost in the New World. Of course it's really an allegory about how this horrible school beats down the underdog, but I'm trying to sail that over everyone's head. You know what an allegory is?"

"Metaphor."

She smiled. "Right. The family is decent but they have no rights. The landlord is a swine. He's dogging the daughter. The cop is corrupt, the teacher is good because that's the only way I could get this past the censors. When you read her lines you'll see she's a total hypocrite. A hypocrite . . ."

"Two-faced."

"Right. Here's a book of old photos, Ellis Island, pushcarts, that sort of thing. Dad, mom, kid, right off the boat."

"You said that already."

"Right. Yellow tabs are girls. Blue tabs are boys. Here's the list."

With five black fingernails, she handed me another of her pink flyers. This one had really nice handwriting on the back. It listed the names of the characters: *Father, Mother, Daughter, Teacher, Landlord, Criminal, Cop*. Across from the characters were names of the actors she'd picked, their measurements, and her costume suggestions. My eyes trailed directly down to *Criminal* to see who got the part. Karl Dingle. Crazy hair. Never combs it. Face like a hawk. Same scrawny kid who burst into tears the first time I tried to borrow a dollar. Total crime kingpin, that guy. Yeah, right. Then I checked the girls. Karen got the daughter role. No surprise. That girl gets what she wants, too. But Madison and Marla were totally shut out.

"Any questions?"

Long pause.

"No? Good."

Longer pause. Luz started to get up.

"Yeah. One question. Don't you think that's a lot of work to volunteer my mom for? This isn't exactly the high school from *Fame*, you know. You've got, like, seven characters and some pretty picky things on your list. Can't they bring their own stuff?"

Luz ran a finger up and down all her earrings and started talking rapid-fire again, as if she hadn't heard me, which I think is what actually happened. Her eyes drifted to the ceiling. "Actors need to feel their character to be their character. You can't become a character in your own clothes. You need a genuine costume. Costumes make the character. Your mom makes the costumes. Tell her I'll even mention her in the program. That'll impress her."

I just stared.

"Look, I've got to go. I've got music class and I'm writing a flute piece for the play." She pushed back her tray of untouched food and took a few steps from the table. "Thanks, Tod," she called over her shoulder.

I didn't say, "You're welcome." I didn't say anything. As I stared into my two bonus lunch trays, I knew I couldn't find the words that meant, "I wouldn't be doing this if your statue had just stayed broken."

With Luz out the door, I looked across the big loud lunchroom to my regular table. None of the guys were there, so I hefted a lunch tray under each arm and lumbered back toward familiar territory. Off my left wing, I spotted Rex and Rob walking straight toward me. I sat right down at a girls' table. The nearest girls slid away from me as far and fast as they could without pausing their conversation. I could almost hear them roll their eyes.

Rex and Rob plopped down next to me. They gave each other a nod, then Rob shot me a big old smile. Not Rex. He was very seriously cleaning out an applesauce cup with his finger.

Rob tried to keep his silent smiley game going, but soon enough he snorted laughter. "Your girlfriend mad at you already? She sure left in a huff."

I didn't bother to answer Rob. I was more interested in what was bugging Rex.

"Is that a fly on your cheek?" sniggered Rob, pretending to look closer. "Nah, it's just black lipstick."

I slapped the table loudly with my palm, pretending to swat that fly. The girls jumped. Then I looked at my hand the way you'd look for a splattered bug. "Missed it," I said.

"I think maybe you got a false eyelash stuck on your eye. You look like . . ."

Rex interrupted without looking up from his little plastic cup. "Seriously, Pops, why is Vampirella in your face all of a sudden? She trying to dig up our crime story for the school paper?"

I rolled my eyes. "Nah. She's begging me to be in her play. Wants me to play some kind of superior criminal mastermind. I was honored, but I told her to bag it. Ain't happening."

"Maybe she'll want me," said Rob, fluttering his eyes and fanning himself with a napkin.

"Maybe when the drugs kick in," said Rex. Then he looked up, straight into my eyes. "Just let's keep away from her. Girls wreck gangs."

Rob got up to leave. He leaned over some stupid girl's backpack and swiped a mechanical pencil that was sticking out. He put it in his pocket, smooth as you please. The girl was lost in a giggle fit with her giggle friends and never noticed.

The bell rang. Rex popped up like a demented jack-in-the-box, tried a layup with his applesauce cup, and totally missed the trash can. To my great surprise, he chose to litter. "You coming, Pops?"

"Nah, you guys go on. I've got a second lunch to finish." Rob fake-tripped Rex twice as they headed out the door. Rex shoved Rob. Once they were gone, I lifted the second lunch tray off *The Illustrated Immigrant* and stuffed the book into my backpack.

Wednesday, November 17

After detention I went home to pick up Mom's old mending. Then I took a bus to the cleaners to trade it for Mom's *new* mending. And her money. Mrs. Tagliapietra, that old and sturdy stuffed gorilla, was thrilled as always to see me. She gets so happy when I'm around that she forgets to talk.

I came in with a thick black plastic garbage bag full of clothes. I could barely see over it. "Where do you want these?"

She scowled and pointed at an old wooden table. I put the bag down on the floor. She kept pointing at the table. I didn't notice. She snapped her fingers and kept pointing at the table, as if it had just started walking.

"Oh, I get it. You want it *on* the table. Right?"

Once I lifted the bag to the table, she holstered the pointer finger on her hip. This is our game every week. Someday I'll figure out how to make her speak to me.

Out came her other hand, cocking a thumb at the back of the shop. That meant, "Your mother's clothes are in the red bin by the back door, and use that door to leave before a customer sees you. Immediately."

I dropped Mom's bill on the counter and put out my hand for the envelope. Palm up. Mrs. T. took her sweet time limping over to the cash register. I can't believe how thick her ankles are. The old register squeaked and rang like a doorbell. The drawer popped open. Mrs. T. glared at the bill, filled a white envelope, slammed the drawer shut, and dropped the envelope on the counter, a foot from my hand. I pinched it between two fingers like they were tongs and lowered the envelope into my carpenter pants pocket.

At the back door, I folded the new pile of clothes and stuffed them into another black garbage bag, being careful not to get stuck on the pins. I can't let the little slips of paper fall off, either. I'm actually pretty careful with my folding, because the women on either end will make me miserable if I screw up.

The back door opened easily once I kicked it. A pin was sticking out and the bag started to slip, so I put my load down on the lid of the little covered trash dumpster to adjust my grip. A red-and-white-striped shirt sleeve was sticking out of the dumpster, so I shoved it back under the lid and took the bag home.

Back at the mansion, I plopped the bag of mending next to Mom's sewing machine. I wondered if this would be a good time to talk to Mom about volunteering her in Luz's army. On the bus ride home, I came up with about fifteen angles. All of them involved really creative lies. They were good lies, but they'd be too much work to set up. Unfortunately, the best route had to be honest and direct. Minus the sphinx, of course. I took a deep breath.

"Damn! I hate sewing!"

That was from Mom, spoken with perfect timing as usual. She was digging through the huge plastic bag with a fury, putting aside the easier stuff for me to do. Good deeds weren't on her mind. Dinner wasn't, either. Hello, macaroni and cheese.

Inside the Crystal Palace, I put new Scotch tape on an old, cracked window. I fiddled with the space heater and adjusted the gooseneck lamp. Stretched out on my bed, I paged through *The Illustrated Immigrant.* It was thick with photos of the good old days, when dentists used hacksaws and "rag man" was a career. All the men wore suits, even the bricklayers. All the women wore fifteen blouses and skirts at the same time. All the kids looked old and dirty and hungry and totally baffled by the man with the camera.

I turned another page. A cop with a wild, walrus mustache was posing next to a gas lamp. How old was he? 20? 50? Everybody looked so old. His black coat seemed pretty fancy, with wide lapels and bright buttons up and down each side. There was white trim along the lapels and cuffs. Where was I going to steal an old-fashioned cop suit? Where would I even find one? I know. At the police museum. No, wait. Bad idea. It's in a police station. Look at all those shiny buttons. Where was I going to be able to boost a dozen old silver buttons like those?

Wait a minute.

What was I saying? What was going on? What did I think I was about to do? Make these costumes myself? I don't know how to do that. What am I talking myself into? What is Luz doing to me? Why am I cursed? Where would I even get the starter clothes?

And then I remembered a certain red-and-white-striped sleeve.

Thursday, November 18

Rap! Rap! Rap! went the knuckles on the window by my head. And instead of getting mad, I was actually glad to have Bernie come by and tear a hole in the dark November morning. It felt like I hadn't seen my old droog in years.

I shook off my cold morning dreams, opened the shade, and looked down on Bernie's scrawny head and red nose as he stamped his feet in our "garden." I'm already a lot taller than he is, but from over the windowsill and under the weak moon, he looked like a three-year-old. I opened the front door, put my finger over my lips—*shhh!*—and led him back into my room.

"Nice toasty room," whispered Bernie. "I'm loving the heater."

"Dick splurged for a really good one after Mom made him give me this heater. The new one doesn't explode even if you tip it over."

"Explode?" Bernie the Brave edged three steps back. In my tiny room, it wasn't possible to go back any farther. If he could have, he would have.

"Chill out, Bernie."

"The big chill, Pops."

"Out cold, Bernie."

"Cold comfort, Pops."

This got us laughing into our hands until we were hissing like snakes. Too bad we still weren't quiet enough for Dick.

We heard The Commander punching the wall to shut us up. I'm too modest to write down the thoughts he shared with us, but I'll admit they encouraged Bernie and me to dash out the door, pronto. I zipped up my coat outside. It was still as dark as midnight.

We didn't wait long for the city bus. I didn't recognize any of the passengers, like I usually do in the mornings. I did notice that Bernie was wearing pale rubber gloves. He had surgical gloves to keep out the cold. I was about to ask where he got them, then I thought twice. Bernie was in a pretty good mood, and I didn't want to bum him out with hospital talk. The news couldn't be so bad if Bernie was here. He updated me on a couple of TV shows and the latest dirt bike news. I acted as interested as I could.

We were making good time. The bus moved quickly. The street outside was empty. We passed a bank clock blinking the time and temperature. That's when I popped Bernie in the arm.

"Ow! Hey! What for?"

"For God's sake, weasel face, it's 5:48," I yelled. "What were you thinking, waking me up at 5:48 in the morning?"

Bernie's eyes and nose were red and watery, but only from the cold. He rubbed his wounded arm while he stared at the floor. "I didn't. I woke you up at 5:22. I couldn't sleep."

"I guess not, you twit." I couldn't think of anything clever to say, so I didn't say anything.

I just crossed my arms and steamed, marveling at how efficient the bus could be when nobody was awake to use it.

I looked out the window. Then I got a brilliant Tod idea

and felt a lot better. So I smiled. Bernie didn't notice. I tried an even wider smile. I said, "Hmm." I said, "Hey!" Nothing. I popped my dimples. I grinned like the Joker. No reaction—Bernie was too busy looking down and rubbing his arm, trying to get my sympathy instead. He wasn't budging. I wasn't either. I tried a chortle, and when it became a cackle, Bernie finally looked up.

"Fine. What?"

"We're getting off at the next stop."

"I'm not walking the rest of the way."

"Yes, you are. We have a secret mission."

He rolled his eyes at me. "I'm not six years old. You'll have to try better than that."

"Fine," I said. "We're going stealing."

Bernie reached up and grabbed the bell cord.

"Why didn't you say so?"

A red light at the front of the bus went on: *Stop Requested.*

The bus sighed and pulled over in front of a corner gas station. I pushed the bar that opened the back door. We hopped down the steps and found 5:53 to be just as dark as 5:22.

I took my natural leadership role. "Follow me."

"What's the booty?" asked Bernie. "Will I like it?"

"You'll see."

We crossed behind the gas station to an unlit alley lined with trash cans. I opened up a can and peered in.

"We're picking trash?" asked Bernie.

"Good," I said. "The garbage men didn't come yet. Let's go."

I counted off the buildings and stopped at the fifth one, a short commercial building with apartments above. No lights were on. The backside alley of the building was surrounded by an old-fashioned picket fence. The fence had a gate, but it was chained shut at night. The pickets (is that what they're called on a picket fence?)

[Sorry, Tod. I actually don't know.]

were three inches wide, with four inches of space between. I felt around for a loose picket, and even in the pitch dark I found one. It slid to the side. Bernie was impressed.

"Eleven inches," I said. "Think you can do it?"

"Sure. What's the buried treasure, captain?" Runty Bernie handed me his coat and was inside the fence before I could answer him.

"Roll that little dumpster over to the fence here. I'll just reach through."

"Push my coat through the hole, huh?" So I did.

The wheels squeaked, Bernie popped open the top, and I started rummaging. "It's nothing but clothes," he grunted. "Exactly why are we hitting the dumpster in your mom's dry-cleaning place? I'm cold."

"Don't get that stuff dirty. Keep it off the ground," I told him. "Toss that cardboard box over the fence."

Bernie heaved the empty box and I caught it. "If this junk's being thrown out, how is this stealing?" Bernie sounded disappointed. "I am *really* cold."

The sun seemed to be trudging past the gloom at last. Through the dim light, and the fence, I sorted what I found into two piles: Possibly Useful and Definitely Not. The red-and-white-striped shirt had a torn collar. It went into my box. So did some kind of velvet dress and a man's suit jacket with a shredded sleeve. A pair of black pants got picked as well. I was interested in a heavy tablecloth that could become somebody's skirt. It was a dark color, either black or blue. Everything else ended up in the Definitely Not Useful pile at my feet.

Meanwhile, Bernie had slipped back through the fence and popped a button. I bent down and scooped up the evidence. Now I'd have to fix his coat again. Maybe I'd fix his ripped-up backpack, too. I went back to my sorting.

"Look, Pops. Heat! Light! All our problems are solved."

While I was thinking about sewing Bernie's coat, Bernie was setting a pile of cardboard scraps on fire.

"Bernie!" I hissed. "You psychopath! Stomp that out before we get arson. Cripes!"

Bernie grabbed my tablecloth and smothered his little pyro creation. Smoke trickled up, but the fire went out. Turns out the tablecloth was green. A light went on upstairs.

I grabbed the box and loudly whispered, "Get out of here, Calvin!" Calvin is one of our fake names. We use it to warn each other and fool the witnesses. We ran down the alley back toward the gas station.

When we reached the bus stop, I was out of breath. Bernie was right alongside me but not at all winded. He weighs only about 40 pounds.

I blew my cool. "You absolute moron. How did you figure we were gonna escape in an alley if the cops came?"

"I didn't really worry about people seeing the fire. I figured it was dark anyway."

Being mad at Bernie is like being mad at a dog. Both of them want to make you happy. Either one will make you crazy. Neither of them thinks of the consequences. And they both smell pretty bad in the rain.

Luck was with us. Another bus came. I held my box as we rambled down the aisle to the wide seat in the back. This bus had more passengers but none in the back. Bernie wanted to sift through the box. I wouldn't let him. But he was persistent.

"You dragged us to your mom's dry-cleaner dumpster. We risked the juvie for something. What?"

"Not the clothes, Flamethrower. The *pockets*. My mom found a gold wedding ring and left it in the pocket. She thought it was a trap from Mrs. T. to catch my mom stealing. Mrs. T. said she'd never seen a ring and she would have kept it herself if she'd known about it. Yesterday, I carried those clothes to the dumpster. I didn't have a chance to check the pockets. Got it?"

This, by the way, was some top-notch, high-speed lying.

Bernie hopped up from his seat. "Tod! You're a genius! Open it! Let's open the box." The bus lurched and he had to catch himself on a pole.

"No way. Not here. Not in public. After detention."

Bernie giggled all the way to school, loving the whole idea

of our master criminal caper. Too bad it hadn't been real. I wish I could really come up with plans as good as that.

When we got to the school, my cardboard box didn't even get a second glance from the guard at the metal detector. She just poked around at the clothes with her wand and waved me through. The stupid box didn't fit in my locker, either. I had to turn it sideways. Then I had to keep kicking the thing until I could close the door.

"Making a new friend, Tod? Oh, it's just a box. Never mind."

That was Mr. Harmon, walking down the hall pushing an A/V cart. He didn't stop.

Who cares if it looks like I was stuffing someone into my locker? I don't care what people think. Looking tougher would be good for business. And business sucks these days when even moneybags Rashawn can't lend me two dollars. A few more solid kicks against the box and I could finally slam the door.

"Pops!"

"Hey, Rex."

"Where you going?"

"English. Where you going?"

"Math. I think."

"Jeez, Rex, it's November. Think you can remember your schedule by now?"

"Where's your English class?

"Right down the hall."

"I don't hardly never come up to the third floor, Pops. The cloud city. They don't let us."

"They don't let *you*."

"You're so gifted. You're so talented. You're so gifted *and* talented." Sometimes Rex likes to beat me up with his own self-pity. Let him. "What's an English class look like where the kids can read?"

"Oh, you know. Alphabet along the wall. *Apple. Ball. Cookie.* And we use desks instead of a rug."

"Oh, looky," said Rex, as we stopped in front of Harmon's room. "Actual sayings from actual writers on your actual door. I love this one—'*The wastepaper basket is the writer's best friend.*' Your teacher wants you geniuses to throw out your homework?"

Class was starting and kids were straggling in the door. Mr. Harmon was setting up the TV on the audio/video cart. One side of the TV was held together with silver duct tape. Ever since we got busted, it makes me uncomfortable. With Rex here in the doorway, it was unbearable.

"Yup," I said. "Up in the cloud city we don't do homework. We just practice tossing baskets with yours. Don't you have Math or something?"

"Science, probably." The bell rang.

"See ya, Rex."

"Your girlfriend in here?"

"See ya, Rex." I ducked in the door and that was that.

I waded down the aisle to my desk in the back corner. Some dweeb was sitting in my preferred chair, and I just stood there until he grabbed his bag and moved. I'm glad I didn't have to look him in the eye.

"Always the diplomat, eh, Mr. Munn?" Mr. Harmon wasn't even looking at me when he said this. He was fiddling with the stupid video machine.

I sat in the still-warm seat and glowered at the empty desk, hands in my pockets, feet shoved under the desk ahead of me. The door opened. It was the Landlord.

"Sorry I'm late, Mr. Harmon."

Five foot five. Twenty-eight-inch leg. Twenty-eight-inch waist. He's going to be the Landlord. In the play, I mean. He's got funny short arms. That's gonna be a problem. I don't know a damn thing about doing sleeves and shoulders.

Anyway, I wasn't kidding. That's what's in the box I brought to detention today. Clothes.

Friday, November 19

Tod, what happened with the box of clothes from yesterday?

Hey! A comment! I figured you'd stopped reading my notebook.

[You've been doing just fine without me.]

About the clothes. I took the long way getting the cardboard box home yesterday after detention. I didn't want anyone I knew to ask me what I had. Guys in my neighborhood have no problem getting in your face if they think you've got something worth having. I don't mean kids my age. I can handle them. I mean the hard guys. The dropouts. I'd have to lie and tell them the box was nothing, and they'd have to tell me to show them, and I'd have to hold the box tighter and they'd have to pull my arms apart while someone grabs the box and runs off a few steps and opens it. Then they'd see it was nothing but clothes, and they'd have to dump everything on the ground and kick it around because they'd be mad at me for not having something good.

They wouldn't hit me for carrying trash, but they'd have to wreck everything in the box and the box, too. They might try to shake some cigarette money out of me, but cigarettes are stupid expensive these days, and they know I don't have that kind of money. Not usually. And if I did have anything like cigarette money, they'd know I'm not stupid enough to be attracting attention, carrying a box. That's why I don't smoke. Too expensive. Too much hassle.

I didn't want to run into my droogs, either. I'd already told Bernie at lunch there wasn't any gold ring in the pockets. He was definitely disappointed. He'd spent the entire morning counting up his share of the money. I knew Bernie would be wondering why I didn't throw away my dumpster treasures out of sheer spite.

Rex and Rob. I just didn't want to see them, that's all.

My mom isn't the kind of mother hen who inspects what I bring home, but why give her something extra to think about? Dick might be curious, but he wouldn't be back from the lawn service until six or seven. He's up to his knees in leaves these days, and on that topic, he still isn't thrilled about my coming to detention every day instead of helping him hoist a rake. I guess he can always hire one of my droogs. They're getting some top-notch experience out there. Except they'd want to be paid.

Thanks for that second note you sent home, Mrs. W. They definitely believe me now. But when exactly is this going to be over?

[We'll see, Tod. Not yet.]

Anyway, it was pretty much dark by the time I got to my block. The streetlights hadn't come on yet. For the second time today I was sneaking these clothes through the dark. What a bunch of work. "They'd better be good," I thought. "I haven't even seen them yet."

Before I went up my front step, I shifted the box so it was pretty much behind my back. I could see through the door glass that mom was in the kitchen, bent over her old sewing machine. The lights were off except for the light from her desk lamp. When I opened the door I knew she wouldn't be turning around.

"Home," I called.

"Yep," she called back.

This was one of those times I was glad for the deep concern Mom showers on me every day. I was in my room in 3.4 seconds, and I closed the door. I put the box down at the foot of my bed and turned on the heater and the light. Then, still wearing my coat, I stretched out on the bed and kicked the box onto the floor.

What was I going to do? Suddenly start sewing costumes? Hide here in my room with a thimble and thread? I stared at my wall. I stared at my rare, imported James Bond poster. I stared at my pile of books I've read fifty times. They all started looking pretty good for the fifty-first time. I stared back at my ceiling, then back at the wall, then back to the poster. I stared out the window, hoping that the light going by was a fairy godmother who did needlework. But no, it was a car. I had used up my miracles on the Return of the Statue. Lucky me.

First things first, I guess. Time to finally open the box. It was looking pretty sad. The box's corners were caved in, half the flaps were nearly ripped off, and the tape holding the bottom together was mostly gone. Once the flaps were all open, my eyes watered with the delicious smell of mothballs and dry-cleaning fluid.

I nearly bit through the toothpick I was chewing. But not from the smell. Turns out none of the things I'd been carrying around all day were worth spit. A blue skirt with a big red stain on it. A pair of bell-bottom pants torn under the fly. A white shirt with ink stains. A padded bra that Bernie had tossed in for yuks. A really scratchy sweater with an alligator bite in it. A wrecked suit coat with a ripped-up sleeve. Finally, there was the torn red and white striped business shirt, which had the initials C.C. III in royal blue across the pocket. It also had a hoof-shaped burn on the sleeve. Mrs. T. must have been gabbing on the phone when she burned this with her iron. I would have loved to hear her explain that mess to C.C. the Third. I would have loved to hear her talk, period. Serves him right for trying to save money at Mrs. T.'s.

I was hoping to find that black cashmere sport coat my mom fixed up. But six hundred dollar jackets don't end up in the dumpster. Just the useless stuff.

I tossed the clothes against the door and made a heap. Then I opened up the small white box I swiped from the miniature golf course last summer and took out one of the little green pencils. On the back of an expired dry-cleaning flyer, I started a list.

1. Dry cleaners
2. Laundromats
3. Locker rooms
4. Where teams practice
5. Coat rooms
6. Parties
7. People's cars
8. Clotheslines
9. Back porches

There had to be more places where clothes can be found. I scratched my forehead with the back of my little pencil. I wrote down one more.

10. Clothes stores

Then I crossed it out. Clothes stores either want money, or they prosecute. Not worth the risk. I drummed on the paper with the pencil and I drew little circles around the numbers, but nothing else came to mind.

"Tod!"

My mom called me from the kitchen, and it wasn't a dinner-bell kind of voice. She had something for me to scrape, wash, lift, pull, drag, or dump. I folded the clothes list and put it in my pocket. The dumpster clothes were shoved away from the door with a swift sideways kick. I turned the doorknob and opened the door. But instead of stepping out of my room, I quickly closed the door again.

"To-OD!" Two syllables. She was getting mad.

What was I thinking? Mom was sure to recognize some of that junk. So I stuffed it back into its dying box and pushed the box under my bed with my foot. Forget dry cleaners. They're always guarded. But laundromats aren't. They're self-serve. I thought about the laundromat two streets away, across from the store that burned. They've got lots of clothes.

"TOD MUNN!"

Mom wanted lugging. Specifically, the lugging of a giant burlap bag of potatoes up from the cellar. In your house, you probably don't try to save money by buying an acre of potatoes at a time. You also probably use some nice warm indoor stairs to step into your cellar. When *you* want potatoes, I bet you just reach in a nice little bag and get some.

In my house, potatoes means putting your boots back on, going out back, shoveling leaves and snow off the cellar door and hauling it open, smelling the wet dirt smell of the basement, clomping down the stairs, swinging your hand around for the hanging lightbulb, grabbing the bulb, turning the switch next to the bulb, stepping over boxes, moving boxes, tossing boxes, and finally getting the thing you want. This time I was smarter than usual. I didn't forget to leave a path out. There's nothing like being in a cold, clammy, creepy, spidery basement holding 50 pounds of potatoes and turning around—only to realize you've blocked your exit path with the boxes you've been shoving around. Then you have to start all over again. Really. You should try it sometime. I'd be happy to trade.

Dinner tonight was potatoes and gravy. My homework tonight was a two-page paper on the Irish Potato Famine. I'm not kidding, either.

When the history paper was done, I changed a bunch of words and I wrote it again for Bernie. Two minutes later, I suited up in my winter gear and went by his house. All the lights were off, and Bernie's phone is shut off, so I dropped the paper through the mail slot. No fair telling our teacher, Mrs. W.

[Do us both a favor and don't mention this sort of thing again.]

[Okay.]

Then I took a stroll down the street to the laundromat. It's a big one, with 40 or 50 machines and nobody working there. After pacing back and forth a few times along the windows, it occurred to me that a laundromat is a public place, and I was allowed to go in.

So I did.

The room was hideous, with plastic chairs that were either Miami pink or Miami green. Two old women were on those chairs, reading gossip magazines, dreaming of a life far from laundry. The TV they were ignoring was bolted to the ceiling, blaring a car commercial, then an ad for a jeweler. When the lottery numbers came on, they both looked up. That's when I cased the place.

Wet clothes in the washer. No. Clothes in the dryer. Maybe. Clothes in a cart. The carts were empty, but sometimes when the laundromat was crowded, impatient people dumped someone else's warm clothes into a cart to take the dryer. Clothes in a cart meant the owner was next door at the bar. That wasn't happening tonight, the place was too dead. I needed a hectic, busy laundromat for ideal clothes shopping. But when was that? When should I come back?

After the lottery balls had all popped into place, I sat down next to one of the old ladies—the friendlier-looking one with the whiskers. She wore a sunflower dress. The clothes in her dryer were a blur of pinks and yellows and light blues. Luz's daughter, Curvy Karen, could use a dress in any of those colors. Unless they had sunflowers, too.

"Good night for laundry," I said, trying to sound cool.

"Yeah? Why's that?" she asked, lowering her magazine,

eyeing the fat teenager who sounded like he was picking her up.

"No crowd."

She snorted a laugh. "Unless you like crowds."

I cleared my throat. "So, um, when's it most crowded?"

"Why you want to know that?"

She was on to me. She knew I wanted one of her dresses for the play. But I stuck with it, trying to find something we had in common. For instance, we were both chewing toothpicks.

"Why?" I asked. "Because I want to know when I shouldn't come to do laundry. That's why."

Did I sound convincing? Was I maybe *too* convincing?

"Lessee," she said, rolling her toothpick from one side of her mouth to the other. "I've been doing laundry maybe fifty years. I'd say you want to steer clear of Sunday night, that's the single men, and most mornings, that's the ladies. Saturday noon, that's the families what bring kids. It's sheer hell on Saturdays. Them monsters will open your dryers early. Dead is Monday nights during football season. You like football? Speaking of dryers, I've got a dress to pull out of here."

I think it's spelled *dryers*, right? Or is it *driers*?

[Dryers]

She hauled herself up and walked over to a bank of dryers. She was a skinny old lady, maybe the same size as Karen Dominick. Exactly the same size, but still totally different.

I noticed when she opened the round glass dryer door, a buzzer went off. This was important. It meant I couldn't just open doors and grab and run. I don't like setting off alarms. Waiting for an abandoned cartload of clothes would be better. But you can't plan for people to sit next door and drink while their clothes get pilfered. It all felt like too much waiting around, too many angry washerwomen, buzzers, the police, etc. The old lady folded a blue dress and laid it into her pushcart. A perfect dress for an immigrant girl. Gone forever. I scratched laundromats off my mental list. As I edged toward the door, she kept her eyes locked on mine.

"Course, the soap machines are usually empty by Sunday. So better you should bring your own."

The old lady clearly wanted to keep handing out her laundry advice. Before I got to the door handle, she put a wrinkled hand on my coat sleeve. Her voice lowered to a gentle hum.

"Why you in a laundromat without laundry, son? You got problems at home?"

My chest got tight and my throat did, too. I tried to think of some words, but I looked in her nice old smiling wrinkly face and the lies just wouldn't come. My eyes started to water up. I don't know why. I wasn't about to let that happen, but I couldn't move, either. Her hand squeezed my arm under the coat and that was even worse. Her eyes were so friendly. I needed to run out of there.

Bam! Bam! Bam!

The old lady and I jumped a foot off the ground. Someone

was pounding on the big plate glass window. Then he pulled his mouth wide with his fingers, stuck out his tongue, and bugged out his eyes. It took me a second to realize it was Rex. He was steaming up the window with his breath. I looked back at the lady and pulled my arm away.

My head was clear again. I tossed the lady an answer as I pushed open the door.

"Nah, my mom says I've got to start pulling my weight. It was either this or dishes. You can't read when you're doing the dishes."

She saluted me like a soldier. "Adios, amigo."

And that's what I say to you, Mrs. W. Adios, amigo. I'll finish this up next time.

Monday, November 22

Tod, was there more to your story involving the laundromat?

There's definitely more. It was a really long day. Remember how I was getting rid of that chatty old lady right when Rex showed up? By the time I got outside and around the corner, the old lady was back on her butt, waving to me through the window. Meanwhile, Rex had written the word *SHOVE* in the fogged glass.

"Pops! What's your scam in the laundry?"

"Nothing. Change machine. Looking for a candy machine."

"Did you tell the old lady you've already got a girlfriend?"

Silence.

"Ready to go make some trouble?" asked Rex.

"I dunno. What you got?"

Rex chortled. "Used car lot? Grocery dumpster?"

"Nah." I'd had enough of dumpsters for one day. Then I got an idea.

"Perfect plan," I said.

"Tell me."

"Owl prowl."

"Now you're talking, Pops. Name the street."

"Let's do the backyards on Chanin Street. No fences."

"Good thinking, buddy."

"Don't *ever* call me that, Rex."

"Sorry, Pops. I forgot."

Rex and I walked the six blocks with our hands in our coats. Soon enough, he pulled out his collection of cigarette butts, picked one from his hand, and lit it. He had a pretty funny story to tell me, which I feel like writing down. And even though the following information is covered in our confidential agreement, I'm leaving out certain details.

Rex told me about a parked car he saw on Such-and-Such Street. "This baby had a jacked-up back end, nice paint, and some extra chrome. Twin exhaust pipes. Car like that has got to have a sound system, phone, something in the glove box, right?"

"Sounds reasonable."

"Even better, there's a nice bag on the passenger seat.

Leather. And no blinking red light on the dash—is that a sweet invitation or what? I step back in the shadows, side up between a house and a big oak tree. Watch the street for a little while. No cars coming, nobody out. No streetlights. This avenue is dead. Dead. I look on the ground, look around, there's half a brick sticking out of the house. I pull it out like I'm plucking feathers. Curl the brick in my hand and ram it through the glass. *Smash!*"

"So you got yourself a new leather bag to carry all your coloring books?"

Rex was smirking. His butt was down to the filter, so he spit it out while he grabbed another crumpled stub and lit it. All in one move. "Don't I wish. Turns out the dude's in the backseat making out with his girlfriend. He hops out with his shirt all unbuttoned, screaming crazy stuff. Hurls that brick right back at me. I did the hundred-yard dash in three seconds. Jumped over a fence and watched him through the cracks. Girlfriend comes out, fixing her shirt. Both of them dressed in black, no wonder I couldn't see them. Don't worry, it wasn't Luz."

At the corner of Chanin Street, Rex started laughing hard, then coughing even harder. Anytime Rex gets excited, he just about swallows his cigarette. He says it's hard to hold a cigarette in place without bottom front teeth. I pounded him hard on the back, pretending I was trying to help him. He was bent over, with his hands on his knees. The knuckles on his right hand were bleeding.

In between coughing fits, Rex finally says, "So I run like a madman ten blocks and find you holding hands with the laundromat lady. Is this a crazy night or what?"

I looked up to the sky and muttered, "Half moon. Half crazy." I was feeling pretty pissed off at Rex. That cop magnet was set to ruin my plans again.

The Chanin Street houses are big. They used to be nice, before the factories closed. Now they're cut up into apartments, with clotheslines crisscrossing the backyards. It was prime turf for stealth shopping, except Rex was announcing our arrival with both lungs.

"C'mon, Train Wreck. Keep it down," I warned him. "Hold your hands over your head. Arms straight up. Just like in the high chair, remember?"

Rex didn't argue. Up went his arms, and he stopped wheezing. "Hey, it works."

"Course it works. And you look so natural. So arresting. All you need is handcuffs."

I slid past a side gate on a chain-link fence. Rex jumped the fence with one hand. Since it was only nine thirty, people were still awake. You could tell which rooms had the TVs because the windows glowed blue. There were a lot of blue windows, with shadows changing across the ceiling. Those houses were the safest bets. TV people aren't about to start looking out their real windows, even during commercials. Not if Rex stayed quiet. I may have mentioned before, he isn't what you'd call predictable. You'd think I'd learn by now.

Behind the first house, I could look down a boulevard of yards all the way to the next block. Fence free. The houses have old-fashioned back porches with rails and steps. Each porch has a pulley wheel that lets you stand still and send your laundry lurching across the yard until it reaches the pulley wheel across the way. November isn't the best month for drying on the line, but that's what we do at my house. I don't know too many people with an electric dryer around here. A few of the clotheslines still had something on them. Even at night.

"Good pickings," I said to myself.

"Huh?" whispered Rex. "Where?"

"Where what?"

"Where are the good pickings?"

"What are you talking about?" I didn't realize I'd said that out loud.

"You are insane," said Rex, who was peeking into a shed. A dog barked, but not nearby.

A couple of houses down from where we started, there was a pair of men's pants dangling from two clothespins. Pants are easy to fix, if I've got to fix them, especially if they're too big. Waists can be pinned, cuffs are a breeze to take up. I'd rather not, of course. I yanked them, and the clothesline made a twanging sound when it snapped back empty.

"Pants?" asked Rex. "Wouldn't you rather have a bike?"

"You see a bike? Because I don't see any bikes this winter. Anyway, I need pants." I bunched up the pants and put them under my coat.

"You look pregnant. Hey, here's a bike," whispered Rex. "Nah, never mind. It's chained."

"Can you blame them? With all the crime around here?"

"I don't know about that," said Rex.

"You should read the police reports. Bad people are out there."

We were halfway down the inside of the block when I saw a dress lit by an upstairs window. It was some kind of blue. Blue or green? No. All blue, and medium-sized, with a frilly square shape sewn onto the front. It looked nice hanging by its shoulders, next to a pair of white stockings. Jackpot. I looked over at Rex, who was up ahead at another house, paying no attention. I gave the dress a tug, but it wouldn't give. Neither would the stockings.

Upstairs, in the lit-up room above my dress, the window was open a bit. A woman was talking loudly with a Spanish accent. Puerto Rican, probably. She was definitely upset, crying and saying, "But why? Why?" over and over. "How can you do this? Why are you doing this?" I stood there listening until the phone got slammed and she was crying full stop. I had already let go of the dress. I decided it looked too modern for the play.

Two driveways later, I caught up with Rex, who was holding a rusted red toolbox. It wasn't a big box, more like the kind your dad gives you for your eighth birthday. A light went on over the porch next door, and we froze. A back door opened.

"Don't you touch my drink," said a lady as she clopped down her back stairs in high heels, holding a big trash bag by the drawstring. Her garbage can lid made a loud metal sound, and she stuffed the bag down with her hand. Once the woman replaced the lid, she looked around. "I don't believe in no ghosts," she called out to nobody in particular. Maybe she saw us, but I can't be sure. The shoes clopped up the stairs and back to her drink. The porch light stayed on.

This all gave me the creeps. "You ready to go?" I asked Rex when we were breathing again.

"Yeah, I got my prize for the night," said Rex. "A pretty red box full of things to throw." It figures that when Rex the mechanic's son looks at a toolbox, he sees an arsenal.

We walked for a while.

"Hey, Rex. How come you know so much Bible stuff?"

He stopped to light a cigarette, and he looked pretty serious, too. Then he started walking again. You might think he didn't answer, but he did. He told me in zero words that he would never, ever tell me. End of story.

My good pal Rex and I don't live very close to each other, so I walked the rest of the way home alone. It was pretty late, and I moved quickly to avoid the real troublemakers in the barrio. The ones who cruise in cars. When I reached my room, I flicked on Dick's space heater instead of my light. The room looked like it was on fire.

I collapsed on the bed. My sheer tiredness crashed in on me. This one long nightmare day had started with Bernie at the dry cleaners at five a.m. and it ended with Rex on Chanin Street well after ten. I'd been all over town, been to dumpsters, laundromats, clotheslines. And all I had to show for it was a pair of pants that didn't even fit me.

Maybe.

I picked the pants off the floor and held them up against my body. Too short. Way too thin. The orange light of the space heater made the pants look black. Blue, maybe. Twenty-eight waist. Twenty-eight leg. No rips. No stains. Bad for me. Good for the Landlord.

Stupid Luz.

I was on my way.

Tuesday, November 23

I could barely get up this morning, and nearly overslept. Bernie, my personal alarm clock, didn't show up. I'm hoping he was just tired and slept in for once. The bus ride was no big deal.

Just inside the main entrance, Greg and Pete and some other kid from the video club had a tripod and video camera set up. My first instinct was to cover my face like an accused felon walking to court. They were taping people as they walked into the school, probably for some genius project. When they saw me, they started singing the little famous part of Beethoven's Fifth—*dee dee dee DUM!*—using my name for the notes, so it sounded like *munn munn munn MUNN!* This in-joke gave them their daily dose of stupid giggles. They knew I wasn't going to answer them in front of the guard. I'm sure they thought they knew why I was steering clear of the camera gear, but they didn't. At least I'm hoping they didn't.

[Your file has been kept confidential, Tod.]

When I was waiting in line at the metal detector, I could feel the sphinx looking over at me with his Potato Head shades and his big old grin. He clearly knows how to have a really good time. Better than I do. While I've been picking rags out of dumpsters, Sphinx has been cruising down the highway with the top down. Sphinx springs back from the dead. Sphinx is magical, and I am cursed.

And then . . . and then I took a closer look. The hubcaps. They seemed different. They were painted shiny black. That wasn't right. I could have sworn they were silver. I'm sure of it. Like Mr. P. H.'s sunglasses, Luz was probably still noodling with her Creation of the Month.

She didn't even know what her statue was capable of. It had the power to wreck my life.

Then something happened. Greg had a sudden hotfoot and tried to rush by everyone to the front of the security line.

"Back of the line," huffed the guard, a strong-looking lady in a police uniform.

"But I've been right here the whole time," whined Greg. "You've seen me."

"Back of the line."

Greg shifted from one foot to the other. "But I've got to go to the . . . I've got to get back into the school."

"You heard me." This woman was no-nonsense in her police hat with the badge. Pity her husband.

Greg the Geek started looking at the kids in the line to find his sucker. I was next at the table, unzipping my backpack, holding it open. He caught my eye and made a face that said "C'mon, be a nice guy, Tod." This desperate weasel had no pride at all, not when he needed something. I had a good chance to make him feel bad, and I took it.

"Hey, guys. Swing that camera around," I called out.

Video Vermin #1 followed my suggestion and swiveled the camera on its tripod. My face flushed. I took a deep breath and faced the camera, trying not to mumble.

"Hey, people, it's Tod Munn. Remember me? Greg here is hopping around because he needs the bathroom. Let's see *that* on the Internet."

I waved my hand toward the metal detector like a hotel doorman. "Greg, be my guest," I said. A few groans came from the kids behind me.

"Great," muttered Greg, which I guess meant "thank you." He stepped in front of me, threw his nice black jacket into the plastic tub, and ran through the metal detector. It beeped, the red light blinked, and the guard made no effort to hide how happy this made her.

"Back through again. Take off your belt." She nearly sang this like a song.

"My belt? I . . ."

"Take off your belt."

"I'm not *wearing* a belt," complained Greg.

"Then what's holding your pants up?" Everybody laughed at this.

Greg rolled his eyes and yanked off his shiny boots with

the shiny buckles. I could see from the perfect writing on the unscuffed soles that they were brand new. He went through the metal detector again with no sounds or lights following him. He grabbed his boots on the other side. Everyone watched him dash down the hall in his socks and vanish into the bathroom across from the main office. Immediately, I put my backpack down in the tub.

"Got it," said Video Vermin #2. He turned the camera back to the door.

Since I don't have new shiny boot buckles, I didn't hold up the line as I stepped through the machine. The guard rolled her eyes at me. I nodded back. It was Greg's turn to be the joke of the hour, and I was in on the joke. Then I picked up my backpack, stuffed my new black jacket into it, and headed to the lunchroom. One good deed deserves another.

They were having cinnamon raisin bagels and scrambled eggs for free hot breakfast today. The eggs looked thin and watery, and I really hate cinnamon raisin bagels, so I grabbed two apples and a couple of milks. On the way to homeroom, I scanned the halls for any contributors to the Tod Munn Snack Fund, but came up empty again. When I passed the candy machine, I poked my finger into the coin return slot, but that was empty, too. I'm sure six dozen other hopeful fingers had already been in that slot this week. I'd survive until lunch.

Today in history I opened the door right after the bell rang, but I forgot to close it. I dumped my Potato Famine paper into Mrs. Carson's half-empty basket and looked for Bernie.

Not there. I looked for a desk in the back. No luck. The last rows were filled with kids who hadn't finished their papers. The only real estate was way up front.

The teacher was fiddling with the taped-up TV on the video cart—the same cart Harmon had yesterday. The exact same cart. It was following me around like Scrooge's ghosts. Mrs. Carson seemed to be having a worse time with the TV than Mr. Harmon did. Her hands were holding red and yellow cables, and she had a pencil tucked behind her thick glasses. Mrs. Carson turned her head to the closest student she could find.

"Tod, could you help me with this, please?"

The TV was sitting on the cable to the video player and she couldn't get it free. The teacher needed someone smart . . . smart enough to lift up a TV. I'm guessing Mrs. Carson doesn't know the terms of my probation. I wasn't in the mood to fill her in, okay? I did the deed, she moved the cable, and boy did I feel useful.

With a clap of her hands and a hup-hup-hup voice, short Mrs. Carson peered over her red-framed, jumbo glasses and addressed the class. "Movie time! Eyes up front, please!" Two dozen kids fluttered papers, closed books, and pushed themselves around in their chairs.

Her voice dripped like a faucet. "As we know, the Irish suffered a series of calamities back home in Ireland between 1845 and 1852. Disease, drought, and starvation. Their experience is the subject of today's documentary. Jackie, please close the lights. And the door."

Jackie got up to close the door, and she turned off the lights, too. I folded my arms behind my head, slid my legs forward, and straightened them under the desk so far they almost touched the A/V cart. I like disease, drought, and starvation as much as the next guy, but I like naps better.

The blue FBI warning came on the screen to scare us from copying the movie. Are they kidding? Then came some previews of other documentaries about disease, drought, and starvation. I guess it's a whole series. Our video began. The narrator had a comforting, low voice. Black-and-white images of farmers and oxcarts and dirty kids flickered on the screen. I knew this already because I already did my paper. My eyelids dragged down. I don't know for how long.

They popped open when a ship's steam whistle blew.

Immigrants!

Here were my costumed friends. My people. The men had scarves around their necks and rough-looking shirts and vests. Their hats were all black. Dick wears an old-fashioned vest just like that. The women had bonnets, ugly big bonnets like the Amish ladies wear at the Saturday market downtown. The kids had the same clothes as their parents, just smaller. I was totally caught up in the pictures, the clothes, and the looks in their eyes. There they were at Ellis Island, nearly in New York City, waiting in line to get their health checked. Official-looking men had already separated them into groups, and were writing on the backs of the sickest and weakest people with chalk. I looked extra carefully at the uniforms these guys wore. They were like cops. Their coats were dark and matched their pants. There were two rows of buttons, big and silver. Greg's coat could fit the bill. The black clothesline pants would match close enough. The buttons could be cardboard. Cardboard covered in tin foil, plastered with glue. I had my cop.

This was the best History class I'd had in a long time.

Next class was Art class. I was supposed to be drawing a bird. Any kind of bird. The only birds I know are the pigeon, the chicken, and the middle finger. Fortunately, tin foil, cardboard, and glue aren't the quality stuff the teacher watches. Luz looked up from her sketch pad and winked when she saw me put the art supplies in my backpack.

In the back of the room, two kids suddenly started singing a TV-show theme. Bird-faced Karl Dingle was one of the singers. He's the dork who gets to be the Criminal in Luz's play. Karl was bobbing his head up and down like a rock star, and his straggly long, curly hair was bouncing everywhere. At the finale, he stretched his long arms high, pumping his fists straight over his head and his skinny shoulders.

Mr. Phister is definitely selective about the kids he bothers to discipline. The ones with talent get his attention. For Karl and his air-guitar band, Phister simply got up and left the room with his empty coffee mug. I looked at Luz, but she was totally focused on making a charcoal sketch of a dragon or something. No birds for Luz's workshop class. I knew Karl's song—at least it would be short.

But no. When the song was done, they started singing it again, this time in different voices, laughing the whole way.

For the sake of Art class, I had to take matters into my own hands.

I sucked in some air. I put my big hands on the long table. I scraped my chair back against the floor. I got up. Luz tipped her head sideways to look at me. So I sat down again in another chair, directly across from the famous play director. I ripped the corner off some scrap paper and wrote my first-ever note to a girl.

He's your actor. Do something.

She read the paper and flipped it over, scribbling quickly and sliding it back across the table.

I'm off duty. What do you want me to do?

The answer was easy.

Fire him.

Luz looked at the note and raised an eyebrow. She blew the paper back across the table at me and went back to her sketch as if I hadn't written a thing.

I guess that left me with the pigeon or the chicken.

Wednesday, November 24

Gym class. Badminton. For God's sake, badminton? Come on, seriously? Every single thing about badminton is awful. The name says it all. I don't know how many other kinds of minton there could be, but even stupidminton has to be better than whacking a feathered rubber ball with dainty mutant tennis rackets.

Mr. Gryzynski teamed Rob and me against two chunky girls. We stared them down through the big white squares of the volleyball net. They were clearly as disgusted as we were to be sharing this moment together.

Rob was swinging his racket like a baseball bat and hopping from foot to foot. "Let's cream them," he cheered. Then he sent the shuttlecock straight into the net and down to the floor.

Nobody moved. After about a week, I walked over to the little dead bird and whacked it under the net, across the floor with my racket. It stopped next to one of the girls' sneakers. Nice shot.

The girls rolled their eyes at each other. The one with the square glasses and short brown hair bent down, grabbed the thing, and straightened her arms. In one slick pivot, she smashed the shuttlecock into the air and nearly into my ear. "One–zero!" said the girl with the baseball cap and the Band-Aid on her nose.

"Yeah, Rob. Let's cream them."

"Girls. I'll show them," muttered Rob. He served back, not exactly realizing that it wasn't our turn to serve. The shot went wild over the wrong net . . . hitting redhead Carrie Donnelly smack on the back of her red head. She turned and glowered at the chunky girls, who muttered something in girl-talk back to Carrie. Whatever they said, it must have worked, because Carrie turned and gave us the lemon face instead. Within seconds, another well-served shuttlecock cocked Rob on the shoulder. "Two–zero!" called the girl with the hat, in the same dull voice she'll someday use for calling bingo numbers.

"Yeah, Rob. You showed them. Why don't we two zeroes just lose and end the misery?"

"Lose? You kidding? I'm no loser." Rob jumped around some more, trying to look like the athlete he isn't. Not by a long shot. He twirled his racket in the air and nearly dropped it. "C'mon. Let's play some badminton!" he called out.

Glasses Girl rolled her eyes even more fiercely. "You gotta send back the ball thingy so we can hit you with it again," she said. "But don't serve it, stupid," added her Band-Aid friend. "It's *our* serve." To make her point, she stretched out the word *our* until it had five syllables.

Rob served anyway. Glasses Girl caught the shuttlecock with one hand, like King Kong snagging an airplane. I seriously thought about quitting and playing on the other team.

"I can't *believe* this is happening to us," whined Rob.

"Look, you want to win, or you want to *say* you won?"

I asked Rob as another featherball flew by. This question actually made Rob stop and think.

"Three–zero!"

"We can tell Rex we won?"

"We can tell Rex, your mommy, your daddy, and your orthodontist that you won. Okay?"

Eighteen serves later, Rob and I were the proud owners of a shutout. The girls grumped at us. "No fair, bad sports," etc., while Rob and I walked over to the wall and sat down.

"Where've you been lately?" asked Rob. He usually gets right to the point. "Rex said he found you in a laundromat, had to drag you out prowling, and all you'd do was snatch pants. Pants?"

I wasn't taking the bait. "You got a problem with pants? Don't you wear pants sometimes, Rob? I know you like free stuff, especially when it belongs to someone else."

"Yeah, Pops, but Bernie says you went and boosted a bunch of clothes from that nasty lady's dumpster in the morning. What gives? Is this got something to do with your girlfriend, Elvira, and her happy little play?

This was all too fast and all too close for me. Better to go full-blast on the offensive than deal with my old pal Sherlock.

"How much allowance you get, Rob?"

"Every week. You know when I get it. I buy the snacks, remember?"

"That's *when*, Rob. I asked how much."

"None of your business, Tod. Enough to fill your fat butt with pretzels, okay?"

"Yeah, well, how many shirts you have to buy with your pocket money, huh, Rob? How many pairs of pants? No answer, huh? I'll tell you the answer. None, Rob. You never bought pants in your life. You got such a sweet deal at home, you haven't even had to steal pants when you wanted 'em. You just ask Mommy."

Rob looked fit to cry or hit me. Or maybe get up and go. But he didn't do any of those things. He needs us too much. I probably should have let up right there, let him have his cry or give me a swat, but good judgment goes out the window when I'm on a roll.

"You know this shirt I'm wearing, Rob? I know you know it, because you've seen this crappy green shirt with the stitched-up collar and the stupid little horse logo every other day for a year. I know you know it, Rob, because you hear all the same stupid jokes I hear. They say, 'The horse's head is in front and the butt is behind it.' They say, 'Munn's practicing for his career cleaning up behind horses.' They say a lot of crap, but they don't say, 'Hey, that shirt is dirty.' You know why, Rob? Did you ever wonder why I wear this shirt every other day, Rob? Because when I'm wearing the blue denim shirt, Rob, this lovely green horsey shirt is drying on the clothesline. So you'll forgive me if I'm not always out shoplifting movies or music or video games to spice up my nonexistent allowance, Rob. I'm trying to diversify my look a little."

Rob's face was a screwed-up puzzle. "You get your money from kids . . ."

Muscle-head Mr. Gryzynski walked over to us, dribbling a basketball, chewing on the rotting red cable that keeps the whistle around his neck. "Okay, ladies, teatime is over," he said in some fake Brooklyn accent. "Back to badminton. Be the first on your cell block to know all the moves."

The so-called gym teacher walked off, aimed his ball at a hoop, and made the shot without hitting the rim. All net. My head swiveled from this inexplicable burst of athletics back to Rob. We were both standing now. I could see his face had changed a little since our discussion began. He wasn't such a pretty boy right now. His eyes looked hard and ugly.

"I get it, Pops. You're too good for your old garbage-picking pals, huh?"

"No, Rob. You actually *don't* get it. You hang out with poor kids because the rich kids won't have you. You're defective or something."

"You think having a dad with a job makes me rich?"

"I think having a *dad* makes you rich."

"Well, you've got a dad, Pops. You just won't . . ."

I don't recall what Rob said next. That's because this is the part where the boring conversation ended and the memorable sword fight began.

I poked Rob in the chest with my racket to shut him up from whatever stupidity he was about to spew. He swung his racket in front of him and batted mine away. He also crushed my thumb with the fat part of his weapon.

"You hit my thumb, Rob," I said, squinting like James Bond

but talking like Clint Eastwood. I brought my sword down against his.

"You fat loser," spit Rob, pushing back, trying to swat me in the stomach with his racket. I blocked each thrust like an expert. The sound of wood on wood was very satisfying.

People started to make a circle around us. Rob and I crossed weapons first one way, then another. Chips of wood flew off our cheap public-school rackets. One of my strings popped. Wherever the teacher was, he wasn't there.

My arms are longer than Rob's, so I had the advantage. I swung back and forth like a sideways pendulum. Rob held me off. Something had to change. Everything I'd ever seen in any swordfight movie was coming to mind. I was trying to remember tricks from *Zorro*, from *Robin Hood*, from *Star Wars*. When Obi-Wan Kenobi fights Darth Vader on the Death Star, he does a fancy 360-degree turn. I did that, and Rob hit me in the back of the head. Kids cheered. I decided to stick with a straight frontal assault.

"That's another injury I owe you," I said, trying to sound calm and in charge while I jabbed at his shoulder.

"You . . . fat . . . broke . . . loser," raged my unworthy opponent, swinging with every word. He was definitely sweating, showing fear. Rob was in this way over his head.

"I'm . . . not . . . a . . . loser," I grunted back.

Click-clack. Click-clack. Click-clack. Swordfighting is actually kind of dull when you're in the middle of it. There's so much back-and-forth, there's hardly any chance for the good guy to skewer his enemy. The way I see it, you've got two basic moves: thrust and . . . something. To thrust is to attack. The other word means to push his sword away with yours. Begins with a *p*. I was doing more thrusting. Rob was mostly *p*-ing.

[The word is "parry."]

I could tell from the way the crowd was opening up that Rob was moving backward. There had to be a wall somewhere to press him against. Now I had a strategy. I was going to play *squash*.

But seriously, where was the teacher?

Rob backed up another step and took a wild swing. He hit my hand hard. I could see my knuckles turn red. I'm sure my face looked the same. I took a few angry steps toward Rob and he stumbled. On his own shoelace, down on the ground, flat on his butt. He pointed his racket at me gamely. With one smooth downward swing I smashed it out of his hand. His racket skittered across the floor into somebody's legs. Suddenly I was the Incredible Hulk and Rob was some terrified rabbit pinned to the wooden floor. I held up my racket over my head, making as if to bring it down on his head. People gasped.

But I didn't do it. I threw my racket hard onto the floor, close by Rob's elbow. What was left of the poor stick broke in half. I had no idea what to do next.

TWEEEEEEET!!!!!

There it was. Gryzynski's whistle. He must have finally gotten back from the bathroom.

"Okay, Zorro. Fencing practice is over," he called, pushing through the edge of the crowd into the circle that stayed open around Rob and me. Rob was still on his back, knees and elbows at sharp angles.

The teacher held out a hand to Rob. "You look pretty pathetic down there, honey. Wanna get up?" Rob took the coach's hand and started to stand. His knees were shaky. He couldn't look me in the eye. Once Rob was standing, he moved toward me. The teacher put his palm against Rob's chest to avoid us starting a rematch.

Mr. Gryzynski's body was blocking Rob, but his head was turned and looking at me as he called out to the entire gym.

"Okay, everyone. Back to badminton. If you want to join our new fencing team, see Munn here after school. Otherwise, don't even think of ruining my equipment."

TWEEEET! went the whistle, right in my ear. People scattered, but fast. Soon only the three of us were in our part of the gym.

Gryzynski muttered to me in a low voice. "I don't see any injuries on your friend here, Munn. You wanna go to the nurse for those knuckles?"

"Nah," I said.

"You could have smashed this little bug, too. Nice restraint. I would have killed him after getting beaned in the head like that. What the hell was that Obi-Wan thing you tried?"

"I dunno."

"Okay, Munn. You head out of here. Go to the nurse, say you fell down. Kids have to see you get kicked out of class or they'll all make trouble. Your friend here can go back and play with the girls. After he picks up what's left of the rackets."

I looked Mr. Gryzynski straight in the eye. "That's it?"

"That's it," he said.

"How come I have to stay here?" whined Rob.

"Because you lost, buddy boy. You have to face your audience alone. Winner walks. Any last words, Munn?"

I thought a second and the answer came easy.

"Told you I wasn't a loser, Rob."

Like Spider-Man after a victorious battle, I walked through the unadoring crowds, straight through the doors.

The End.

Thursday, November 25

Yesterday after detention I wandered over by the courtyard to see about Rex. By this time, garbage duty would be nearly over, and Rex would have gotten an earful from Rob about the Big Bad Badminton Battle a few hours earlier. That wouldn't be good for me. It's important to be the first person to deliver bad news. For Rex, having two of his droogs rip it up would be bad enough. To do it in the gym, in a very public, very nasty (very cool) swordfight, would be the worst kind of news. Rob and I would both want Rex to take sides. Different sides.

I wasn't worried about Bernie. Here's why:

1. I knew Bernie first, before anyone else. I met him in first grade when Mom and Dad sentenced me to this run-down neighborhood.
2. Around fourth grade I taught Bernie how to explore parked cars to see if they were locked. *Treasure chests*, we called them, full of CDs and pocket change. Bernie built up a totally random CD collection thanks to me.
3. When I got big and tall in sixth grade, I found myself protecting runty Bernie from the low-grade bullies who hit kids for fun, not profit. He'll remember that.
4. Neither Rex nor Rob will sit and listen to his endless daydreams about motorcycles. Or if Bernie talks about his mom being sick, Rex tells him to stop whining, everyone's got problems. Rob just gets squeamish and changes the subject.
5. No, I wasn't worried about Bernie.

But Rex is a different story. We're losers together. *We don't care*. We're like freedom fighters. We've been getting revenge against lucky kids like Rob for the last couple of years. It's our way of making things even, at least while we can.

There is one huge difference between Rex and me. He can't see that he's going to be in this slum his whole life. He's blind that way, pushing up against the system like a rat who doesn't know the maze is rigged.

Like, Rex is always talking about how he doesn't need

school because someday he'll open a garage like his dad. A couple of times he's had the brass to steal tools from back behind another guy's garage. No problem there. But does he save the tools for when he gets his own shop? Does he even give them to his dad? Not likely. Rex trades them for cigarettes. He doesn't *think*.

He'll probably take a swing at a cop one day, when just plain talking would have saved his butt.

After a couple of weeks together, stuffing soda cans and blowaway homework pages into trash bags, Rex might just decide that some of Rob's future salary could rub off. His dental work, too. And if Rex is forced to make a choice, I can't say for sure which way he'll go.

Anyway, Rex wasn't anywhere to be found.

I went back to my locker to get my coat. There was a black-and-white checked envelope taped to the door. The stationery inside also had black and white checks around the border. The whole thing looked like the floor of an ice cream parlor. I wouldn't need two guesses to figure out who it was or what she wanted. I read the note anyway.

TM: Please thank your mom for me. —L.

How's that for class? No mention of the purpose of the letter. No incriminating comments for a stranger to read. And if you weren't having a nervous fit keeping an idiot promise about a stupid play, you might even think she was being no pressure at all. But I knew better.

On the bus ride home, I stewed over my situation. Here it was Wednesday, and Luz needed the costumes for the play next Friday. She wanted dress rehearsals for at least two days, so I had a week at the most. Just seven days to lift the curse of the Sphinx.

I pulled *The Illustrated Immigrant* out of my backpack and flipped through it, starting from the back. The little blue library card popped out—the book was due back on Monday, and I hardly had any clothes. As if I didn't have enough other crap to think about.

On page after page, all I could see were guys wearing Dick's vest. It didn't matter what they did for a job—ditch digger, pushcart pusher, pickle pickler—everybody wore vests. And hats. Forget the hats, Luz. Finding the clothes is hard enough.

Speaking of ditch diggers, outside on the street there was some kind of construction work with jackhammers and gas company trucks with yellow flashing lights. There weren't any police cars, so I didn't suspect terrorists. Just rotting pipes. The flagman made our bus take a funny detour down a different one-way street. And my never-fail Tod luck played itself out perfectly. I'll explain.

We passed a gas station. We passed a building that had gotten partly knocked down. We passed an empty lot. Then we passed the Helping Hand Thrift Shop. My own helping hand grabbed for the bus's *Stop Requested* bell as soon as I saw the two huge metal containers overflowing with donations. The bus stopped three blocks later. Time to rock and roll.

The Helping Hand shares a shopping plaza with an empty liquor store and a beauty salon. It's set back from the street by a narrow parking lot that could hold about ten cars, side by side, in front of the stores. Most of the parking spaces were empty. There was broken glass on the blacktop. Next to the thrift shop was a chain-link fence with plastic green stuff woven in so you couldn't see through it. The fence had a gate, but the gate was open. Inside this little area were the two drop boxes I saw from the bus.

Scattered around the front and side of these containers were a whole lot of cardboard boxes with clothes and shoes and board games and blenders and stuff. The thrift shop was closed, and from the looks of things, it hadn't been open for a few days. That would explain why all those cardboard boxes were there. Anyone who'd be charitable enough to make a donation would probably be scared of the neighborhood—too scared to leave their car long enough to put the donations in the containers. Lucky me.

Even luckier was the fact that the drop-off area was lit by a floodlight on the roof of the Helping Hand. A bright one. I could actually see what I was doing out in the cold.

Where to start? The wide-mouth chutes on the containers were set up so you couldn't just reach in. That left the cardboard boxes. Some of the boxes were strictly appliances and old alarm clocks. I poked in a shoebox and found an old wristwatch, the kind you wind up. I put it on and set it to 5:15. That would be about right.

One box looked especially promising, because it was wide

open and had an old man's shoes on top. Shoes weren't on my shopping list for Luz, but I figured there'd be men's clothes underneath. I piled the shoes to one side of the box and found a couple of suit coats. A black one and a brown one. Neither of the coats had vests, but they were clean. I held the coats up against my body. One was long and thin. The other was for a short skinny guy. I dug back in my bag and took out *The Illustrated Immigrant*. The list with the actors and the costume suggestions Luz gave me was still tucked between the pages. I checked these coats against Dad and Landlord—they looked good—and I checked them off the list.

Then I looked around for a place to put the suits down. I picked up a brown fake-leather suitcase, but it smelled so bad I tossed it behind one of the metal containers. Under it was another bag, a jumbo floppy vinyl duffel bag. Unfortunately, it was bright purple, with *Escape!* written in huge pink letters, and the name of a cruise ship company underneath. I didn't want to carry this horribly girly bag, but I guess any old port in a storm, right?

Soon enough I found out a lot of the boxes were useless. I stacked all those cartons neatly to one side. Stained baby clothes and chewed-up baby toys were in huge supply. A really heavy box had rusty tools like wrenches and a crowbar. Why don't people just throw this junk away? Does it make them feel better to use the Helping Hand as a guilt-free dumpster? Too bad I don't like jigsaw puzzles. There were lots of those, too. Probably missing pieces.

It wasn't until the 4,000th box that I found some women's

clothes. Most of this garbage was incredibly ugly. Big buttons, zigzags, huge wide white lapels. I guess if you'd buy this hideous stuff in the first place, you're crazy enough to think someone else would want it, too. But I found a long skirt and a blouse that weren't so bad. Also, there was an apron and a pair of white stockings with a hole I could fix. A lot of those old-fashioned women in the photos wore white stockings.

My new purple *Escape!* duffel bag was getting more and more clothes folded into it. When I found a near-enough size and style for a character, I crossed it off the list. This was excellent. Characters were actually getting *crossed off the list.* And I could cross off this idiotic commitment forever. I was close to done.

Suddenly I found myself being pummeled by a seriously bright light. A car had pulled into the parking lot and was pointing its halogens straight at me. I couldn't see who was in the car. A new Volvo. Whoever it was wasn't in a hurry to get out. I decided to ignore them. That is, until the horn honked. I just about jumped out of my skin. But as a special favor, I turned my head toward the headlights.

A power window went down. "Young man?"

I could tell it was an older lady. I could tell what she was thinking, seeing me huddled over all these boxes. And I let her keep thinking it. I wiped my hands on my pants and started toward her.

"Yes, ma'am?"

"I have some boxes and a vacuum cleaner in the trunk. Will you get them, please?"

"Yes, ma'am." This had to be worth two bucks. Maybe three.

I went around the back of her car and the trunk released with a gentle *click*. Once I had the trunk open, I could hear nice classical music from the back speakers. Her trunk was incredibly clean. She had a bag of yarn and a snow brush and some antifreeze. She had two good-sized boxes and an old chrome canister vacuum cleaner, the kind they stopped making 30 years ago. More guilt-free junk disposal. I could have hauled all three things at once, but that would have looked like less work.

After the third load, I stood by her window waiting for my tip.

"Thank you, young man. May I have my receipt, please."

You'd think having a new Volvo would free you from need. Like, the need to save ten bucks on your taxes.

"Sorry, ma'am. They're all gone for the day."

She looked sorely disappointed, like she was going to ask me to put the boxes back into her trunk. Then she thought better of it.

"Yes. Well, I see. Thank you very much."

She started powering her window back up, and I started imagining how her rear window would look with a chrome vacuum cleaner sticking halfway through it.

Maybe she could read minds. Because the window opened again, and she smiled a nice old lady smile. "Well, that's not your fault they're closed, is it? Thank you very much, young man." She held a five-dollar bill between two wrinkled fingers and it fluttered in the wind. I took it in my gloved hand and touched my other glove to my ski cap, like a sort of polite salute. Five bucks! That's a buck for each box, and two more for nearly getting stiffed on the tip. Guilty people always overpay.

Once she was back on the street, I didn't miss her headlights one bit. I walked over to her boxes, but they were only filled with magazines. The name on the subscription label was Evangeline Peabody. Figures.

I sorted through the last few boxes, and then there weren't any more. I still had some women's clothes to collect—for instance, the girl playing the Teacher is kind of fat and I didn't find anything good to fit her. The boxes were done and that was that. My new watch said 6:30. I couldn't believe I'd been there over an hour. I mean, if the watch actually worked. It could just as easily have been four in the morning. Weirdly, I wasn't cold or hungry at all.

The big duffel bag was filling up. I guess I could have been more grateful for finding as many clothes as I did. Two hours earlier, I'd had nothing for the play but a pair of pants and Greg's jacket. Now I had nearly everything I needed. It's just that when a miracle happens, you want a *complete* miracle to happen. Why not, right? That probably explains why I was feeling bad enough to kick the side door of the bigger metal container. And the door wobbled. And a single, beautiful image filled my mind.

The rusty crowbar.

I tore into my neat stack of boxes. I pulled one after another off the pile. I opened all the flaps I'd tucked tightly into place, and then I pushed the unwanted boxes aside. When I finally found the tools near the bottom of the heap, I realized how heavy that box had been. I could have saved a lot of time searching by weight. In my hurry to find the crowbar, the boxes became just as messy as when I arrived. I vowed not to waste any more time being tidy.

The crowbar really had a lot of heft. I don't think Ricardo, Rashawn, and my other deadbeat friends would feel so brave stiffing me if I carried this. I slapped one of my palms with the rounded end of the crowbar. Bits of rust flaked off onto my glove. Too bad I couldn't bring this baby to school. The metal detectors might maybe possibly detect it.

Now, I don't know about you, but I've never really thought much about the locks on clothes donation bins. Turns out they're pretty lame. Still, it took a lot of prying to get the crowbar wedged between the door and the frame so I could pop the lock. Both the door and the frame bent from the pressure. Back and forth went the crowbar. My badminton knuckles started to hurt. Metal creaked and moaned and was far too loud. I'm sure what I was doing was a crime. Even so, it's hard to imagine getting busted for stealing free clothes.

I leaned all my weight into the crowbar. The metal screamed louder, louder, and then the lock popped off with an explosive *KRUNK!* The frame around the door was sort of wrecked by now. That door wasn't about to close again. Not without the help of a welder.

But man, what I found inside! Clothes galore. Stuffed into

big garbage bags, pressed together like sardines, smelling way too much of mothballs and hairspray and poverty. But the harsh floodlight on the roof told no lies—there were plenty of dresses to be had. Frilly and colorful bits were poking out from every direction. I wish I'd thought of hitting this container first. The boxes I'd been digging through were a waste of time compared to the goodies inside. How'd so much stuff accumulate out here? Maybe I really was the store's only employee.

I hauled out a few bags of belts and purses and other useless junk. Then I found a yellow plastic bag with real promise. The shiny red shoes at the top of this bag were as wide as car tires. I smelled a fat lady's clothes, for sure. (Not literally.) I dug down inside the bag. Right on top I uncovered a heavy green coat, then one of those navy coats with only one silver button attached.

Too bad there weren't more buttons. It was just what the cop needed. Even though it was a woman's coat, it was much better than Greg's jacket. I folded the navy coat and put it in the purple bag. My list was almost done. I needed to find just one more thing. Then I could *Escape!*

A second, identical yellow trash bag held the final treasure. Inside was a wide, pale pink dress with white circles on it. Perfect for a frumpy teacher. Easy to hem. I held it up to my shoulders to check the size, and I turned around toward the street to look in the light for stains.

Another set of headlights attacked my eyes. Another tip. Lucky me.

Someone yelled "Hey! Tod!" and I squinted into the high beams. There was a guy in the darkness standing on the sidewalk. He was aiming something at me. It looked like a gun. Why would he want to shoot me? How did he know my name? The laughter confused me even more.

"Oh, God! Munn in a dress! It keeps getting better! Totally priceless!"

What . . . was . . . going . . . on? My mind slowed down. Had . . . to . . . think. Shadowy figure, probably about my age. Laughing. I froze completely, trying to get my eyes to focus in the bright headlights. I didn't move. I didn't even lower the dress from my shoulders.

"See you in school, Mrs. Munn!" said the voice.

The car door opened. Its inside lights went on. I didn't know the driver, a blond guy. Maybe 20. But I knew the passenger hopping in, holding a video camera. It was Greg, in a new coat. President of the video club. Spelling bee cheater. Undercover terrorist.

Their car shifted into reverse, then took off with a roar. By the time I reached the street, waving the dress like a lariat, they were already burning rubber around the corner.

I had plenty of time to process all this while I packed up. My mind was speeding because I know what Greg is capable of doing with a video like that. But how did he find me? And what does Greg really want from me? Besides his coat, I mean. I pulled the sides of the big duffel together. The zipper was strong for an ugly giveaway bag. So were the handles.

Fortunately, things weren't all tragic. I had all my clothes for the play. Everything but the vest. I hefted the duffel bag onto my shoulder when a city bus approached. I waved and waved, and the driver had enough heart to stop between stops on a cold night, even though I looked like the rest of the homeless, moneyless folks around here. I almost felt like giving him my five dollar tip. Almost. He even let me use my school pass way after school hours.

Question: What were the chances that I could get that vest from Dick?

Answer: Zero.

The lights were on in the kitchen when I stomped up my front step. From the dark, cold street, through the front door window, the house looked almost homey. When I turned my key and stepped inside, the whole place smelled like a giant sweat sock. Dick was in the back, standing at the stove, using our biggest pot. I shed my coat and quickly put the cruise ship luggage next to my bed. It would never fit underneath. I closed the door tight. Then I sauntered back to where the action was.

The pot was bubbling. Dick was tasting from a wooden spoon as he looked up at me. The electric wall clock said 8:20. It is an hour fast. Nobody's changed it since daylight savings ended. So it was 7:20. My new watch still said 6:30.

Dick put the pot lid back on. "Home so soon?"

"Half day," I said.

I looked around and saw it was quiet. Too quiet. I got the sudden, uncomfortable feeling that Dick and I were alone in the house. Time alone with Dick was a problem that had to be avoided. It could lead to anything—lawn care commitments or, worst of all, a conversation. I moved a few steps back.

"Mom home?" I asked.

Dick lifted the pot lid again with one hand and went back to stirring his potion with the other. For no reason, he suddenly looked more like a cop than a gardener.

"She's out looking for you."

"Really?"

He smiled, sort of. "Of course not. She's picking up a rush order at the cleaner's."

"She mad I wasn't here to do it?"

"You're a big boy. She's a big girl. You're both allowed out at night." He took another sip from the stinkpot. "Don't sweat it. It's good for her to get out sometimes."

"Yeah. Yeah. I guess." I sounded like an idiot. I started to head back to my room when I stopped and turned back.

"What are you doing, your laundry?"

Dick laughed at this. Genuinely laughed. "Yeah. Still not enough soap for my taste. It's boiled cabbage, you dope. You want some? Nah, never mind. I know all about you and vegetables."

Actually, I was starving. "What's it taste like?"

"To tell you the truth, I can't really say," said Dick. "I guess it tastes like memories. Grandma Maloney's pink kitchen. My old man's bar friends. Cleaning dinner trays in the army. Back in the day, bars had a steam table. They served corned beef and cabbage to the working stiffs. Not your damn chicken fingers."

"Chickens have fingers?" I asked. Joking.

"Hard to say," said Dick, not seeming to get the joke. "Last I looked, chickens didn't have fingers. Don't have nuggets, either. Wings, sure. But fingers? They're like nuggets. Probably You-Know-Who owns the word *nuggets*. So the rest of us get the fingers." This cracked him up, and he didn't stop laughing until his next sip of cabbage soup from the wooden spoon.

It was my cue to leave. I grabbed the bag of crackers we got in the bulk grocery section and took it back to my room.

"Hey, leave me some crackers!" Dick called after me. "Cabbage is almost ready!"

"Homework," I muttered. As I opened the flimsy hollow door of my room, I also said, "thanks." I even said it out loud. But I'd be amazed if he heard me.

For once, I wanted to be in my room. Aside from the crackers and Dick in a good mood, there was a big, ugly, purple bagful of good luck waiting for me. I pulled the knobby, dangling metal chain and the overhead light went on. For some reason, my dinky room didn't look so bad. Not with my clothes homework mostly done . . . and filling all the available walking space. Now I just had to sew a little. As little as possible.

After the hunt, that would be the easy part.

To sort of savor the moment, I waited before digging into the crackers. Or the purple bag. It was the ugliest thing I'd ever seen, but it was an actual suitcase that had actually been on a trip somewhere. Not like the lame luggage under my bed. And now it was mine.

My eyes wandered over to the stack of shelves in the corner over my bed. Bottom shelf, my cigar box full of scratched and scrapped lottery tickets. Middle shelf, the mug with my pen collection. Top shelf, the baseball trophy I found in Dave Simon's bedroom. I used to keep that apology letter from Dad in the cigar box, but I moved it to the suitcase when I got tired of looking at it. My spelling bee certificate is in there, too. I didn't want to think about that right now. Or Greg.

After that, I looked at this detention notebook poking out of my backpack, and I was glad I took it home for the weekend. All this stuff couldn't have waited until Monday afternoon.

Next I looked up at my prized poster. And James Bond looked back down at me from behind his pistol. I read the slogan for the thousandth time: "His bad side is a dangerous place to be." James and I can identify with that, especially if we haven't had something to eat in a while.

And finally, I took a good, long look at the bag of crackers.

P.S. As I expected, cabbage tastes awful. But Dick let me borrow the vest.

Sunday, November 28

Mrs. W., if you don't mind, I'm going to spare you and me most of the details of taking a bunch of clothes thrown away by privileged folks in the twenty-first century and mutilating them to look like the clothes of underprivileged folks from the nineteenth century.

But here are a few highlights from my weekend anyway:

On the first sewing night, I had to tiptoe into the kitchen after Mom and Dick went to bed. It was weird. I haven't tiptoed around the house since grade school—there's no reason—but I needed to get thread, scissors, the measuring tape, a couple of thimbles. Good thing about the thimbles. I probably poked my fat thumbs five dozen times, especially pushing the needles through the thicker clothes. A few other times I had to go back out at night and borrow more sewing stuff. Like the heavy, C-shaped upholstery needles I used for the men's coats.

The pieces of the costumes were all there. At first I found Luz's list to be way too detailed and way too controlling, and it kind of pissed me off. But when I had my bed completely covered with castaway clothes, her uptight list came in handy. I could just check sizes for each kid. Check them off. And move on.

The Mother's dress needed a flat square in front. I cut a piece out of an enormous woman's blouse, sewed it on, and let a lot of stitching show. In the old-fashioned times they sometimes made huge stitches, like they were sewing with horse bones or something.

The Landlord wears black, which was fine, but his jacket was a problem. According to Luz's notes, the jacket I had found was too long for the arms of the jerk playing him. I wasn't sure how to shorten the arms, so I had to sneak back out at night and grab a coat of Dick's that Mom had performed the same surgery on. I took Dick's coat into my room and turned it inside out but Mom's really good and I couldn't figure out the trick to keeping the stitches hidden. Too bad for the Landlord. I kept him in stitches. Big ugly stitches. I used dark thread so you can't tell from row LL that I did a hack job.

Mr. Landlord was also supposed to have a gold pocket watch on a chain. According to the author, he pulls it out and says, "You got one hour to pay me the rent." I'd call the pocket watch a prop, not a costume, but here it was on the list and there's no arguing with Luz. The gold chain was the easy part. I've had a fat one in my suitcase for two years. Me, I don't wear chains, so nobody will think it's mine. Plus, the kid I got it from was at another school. It's the watch that had me worried. I mean, until I was making spaghetti on Saturday. The lid from the jar of sauce is shiny and gold. A little glue and a fat marker got me a watch and chain. It'll even fit in Dick's vest. I measured the pocket.

I wanted the Father to have a vest, too. This bugged me for a day until I got a pretty good Tod idea. A vest is a jacket without the arms, right? So I dragged out the messed-up sport coat with the ripped arm from Mrs. T.'s dumpster, ripped off both arms, neatened it up, and it didn't look bad. I had to make the waist a lot smaller, and I didn't really know how to do that. I was tempted to use a stapler. The Landlord ended up with the black pants I got from the clothesline that night. The size was exactly right.

The Daughter's dress wasn't a particularly nice dress. In fact, it was downright ugly. Too bad. The size was right, and Karen can make even a potato sack look pretty good. I cut the sleeves and collar off the red-and-white-striped shirt I got from Mrs. Tagliapietra's dumpster and made a nice head scarf for Karen to wear. If Karen has anything to say about her wardrobe, she can take it up with the director. That's not my department. The dress I saw hanging on Chanin Street the other night would have been a lot better.

Another problem. Karl Dingle's coat looked too wide for his scrawny chicken shoulders. But according to Luz's notes, it was fine. I think Luz was off by about six inches, which is a pretty huge mistake. Luz is going to have to get me a new measurement. That's not my department, either. Meanwhile, I tore out the labels and changed the buttons so Greg couldn't identify his old jacket. Too bad it didn't fit me.

Last entry for a Sunday night: The clothes smelled kind of bad once they were in my room for a while. But laundry wasn't on my list of obligations to the Sphinx. Good thing my room is so well ventilated. I kept anything I wasn't working on sealed in the purple bag. No matter what I tried, the bag wouldn't fit under my bed. And I sure wasn't moving my secret personal suitcase to make room.

I was just about done. Tonight Mom asked if I had her measuring tape and I made up some excuse. I told her I was practicing making nooses so she'd believe me. She didn't get mad or even tell me I should work on something more modern, like electric chairs. She's acting kind of weird this weekend. She even asked me if I'm feeling okay. Except for that turkey dinner Thursday in the Roadhouse Diner, with the stuffing and cranberry sauce and two big slices of pumpkin pie, I pretty much spent the whole four-day weekend working in my room.

Monday, November 29

Today was a rainy, gray, cold, drab Monday morning. No Bernie. I have no idea how he's going to keep from flunking everything. I was pretty close to soaked by the time I got to school.

That stupid sphinx was waiting to pounce on me at the front door. Too bad for you, Sphinx. I've got your number, Sphinx. I'm winning, Sphinx. Tomorrow—or maybe Wednesday—I'm making the handoff to Luz. I'll close out the clothes. And the miserable month of November will be over. There will be a new Artist of the Month. And it won't be Luz. And you'll be gone. Gone, gone, gone. The statue of limitations will be finished. And me and my afternoons and my friends will be back to normal.

Stupid curse.

For instance, I went to the library first thing this morning to check the computer. Mrs. Culpepper didn't want to let me sign on when it wasn't my official time. But Mrs. Lent gave me a password anyway. I put on the headphones and logged on. Just as I expected. The Internet sucks. I hate it.

[Why, Tod? Would you please elaborate on this for me?]

[No way.]

Finally, it was lunchtime. I headed over to my usual lunch table, figuring that Rex would have talked some sense into Rob by now. I'd been giving it some thought and I'd decided to laugh at the Raising of the Rackets and forgive Rob and let him stay in the gang. (I mean droogs. It's *not* that kind of gang.) We'd make plans for our next big thing. Make it all go away so I wouldn't have to do it myself. For my part, I brought along my new deck of cards I got at the Roadhouse Diner and a bag of licorice pieces (red, not black) that I was even going to share with my droogs.

But they were gone. All of them. Bernie was probably at the hospital. Where were Rex and Rob? Even worse, three little pink idiots were sitting in our seats, arguing over a deck of Japanese Robot trading cards they'd set up across the fake wood tabletop. Things were definitely getting out of control.

I caught myself scanning the room for Luz. I don't know why—probably to tell her to call off her sphinx, or maybe I'd mention that the costumes were almost ready.

After walking about halfway around the edge of the lunchroom, I heard a burst of laughter. Maybe Principal Carnivore had just slipped in yogurt? No, it was just the people from the play "doing" lunch. And dead center, completely surrounded by her actor gang, was Luz. Karen wasn't there, of course. But the rest of them were throwing a party in the middle of the lunchroom. It sure seemed like they wanted everyone on the outer edges to feel bad about not getting an invitation.

Who cares? For the rest of the week they'd be the In Crowd. They'd get their costumes, their dress rehearsal, their show, their applause. After that they'd hand in reports, take their exams, and break for Christmas like the rest of us. Come January, no one will remember. They'll be just the same old bunch of losers in the worst school in town.

A couple of the world's greatest actors saw me standing there and whispered to each other. Karl Dingle, the singing criminal genius, was the loudest. He was even brave enough to point at me before making some comment and crumpling into a hysterical fit with the dweeb playing the Landlord. I kept my eye on Luz. She didn't see me, or she would have shut those idiots up and waved hello.

Eating alone is no big deal. I grabbed a school newspaper from the pile and sat down to count the spelling mistakes while I downed my grilled cheese and coleslaw. Big mistake. The front page of our crapola paper was all about the play. There was a weird photo of Luz, shot from below by a midget with a camera. The effect was creepy. She was posing with one eyebrow raised like she was Mr. Spock's Vulcan sister. Her eyeliner was especially thick. The rings in her nostrils looked huge. So did her nostrils. Luz was standing in front of the sphinx, holding her flute like a baseball bat. I don't know when the photo was taken, but I sure noticed the hubcaps. They were the way I first remember them, silver and shiny. Not black. And the sphinx had a more square head. ~~Like Mr. Gryzynski.~~

I dumped my tray in the trash. A quick inspection trip to the front entrance confirmed that there was, in fact, a mystery to solve. How did the sphinx die and come right back to life *and* change a little? I don't know. The whole school's a kiln. Maybe the heat keeps changing the paint. I flipped to the back of the newspaper, where all the contributors were listed. Guess who's the editor of the paper?

And one more thing I figured out. She set the camera on the floor, set the timer, and took the picture herself. I just know it.

The only thing she can't do is sew.

Turns out the silver police buttons weren't too hard to make after all. First I arranged 12 wide-mouth bottle caps that were scrounged from the lunchroom recycling bin. Then I took the tinfoil I boosted from art class, smoothed it out, and cut it into 12 squares. When I glued the foil onto the bottle caps, the squares became circles. But Tod, you ask, how did you get the buttons to stay on the jacket? And I answer, "Because I am an expert and a genius." I glued paperclips onto the backs of the buttons so they could be sewn on. It took me one whole Math class to make the twelve buttons. Don't worry, Mrs. Woodrow. It was a substitute teacher. After she received my Neanderthal stare-down from the back of the room, this lady would have let me take out a welding gun and an iron mask.

And why, you ask, did I need to make them at school? And I laugh and say, "Because I'm a criminal mastermind, that's why." I knew I couldn't get past the metal detector with the bottle caps and paper clips. And I wouldn't be caught dead with the costumes. So I set 'em up in school. The jacket was smuggled into school in my backpack. My plan worked perfectly. And since we've agreed this is my safe room, Mrs. W., I'm going to put this pencil down right now and start sewing those beautiful buttons right onto that smelly coat.

Tuesday, November 30

*** MRS. W.—IMPORTANT NOTE AT THE BOTTOM. PLEASE READ IT TODAY BEFORE DETENTION THIS AFTERNOON. —TOD

Hi, Mrs. W. I figured since I had Study Hall this morning—and I hadn't finished writing about yesterday—you wouldn't mind if I came by your office in the morning to pick up the notebook. You sure looked surprised and happy. It is SO easy to manipulate adults.

There are three things I didn't mention when I was writing yesterday, for two different reasons. First was that I was walking to class and saw Karl Dingle in the hall. I'm sure he knew that I'd seen his comedy act in the lunchroom. Everyone's got something to say at this school. But Karl the Master Criminal really peeved me. He tried to ignore me. I didn't return the favor. I grabbed him by the shoulders and pushed him up against a locker pretty hard. I straight-armed him and didn't let go of either shoulder. His eyes begged "don't hit me" while his mouth said nothing, for a change. I didn't want to get suspended or anything, so I merely leaned in, real close, and gave him my best snarling voice.

"Your singing sucks."

"Sorry," he squeaked.

"Go."

I released his shoulders from my grip, but my hands stayed firmly in place against the lockers. He bent his knees a bit, snuck under the tree branches of my arms, and ran off like a girl.

Good thing my hands get sweaty. I pulled out my mom's measuring tape from my pocket and measured between my handprints. Eighteen-inch shoulders. I was right. Luz had gotten it wrong.

So I didn't mention this because I'm getting kind of tired of writing down all the crappy things I do to people and having you read it. But then I realized hassling Karl Dingle was for a good cause, so I put it in anyway.

The second thing I didn't mention was something I still feel weird about. I did see Rob in the hall after lunch, and his face got serious and he avoided looking in my eyes, like he was in a hurry or something. He was still sore, and that wasn't good news. And I didn't see Rex all day, except out the window of detention while I was sewing the buttons. He and Rob were in the courtyard. Still no Bernie. Rex was holding the big black trash bag while Rob was poking papers with a stick. I told you Rex was smart. He had Rob doing the real work.

I haven't seen them this morning, either.

The third thing was maybe the weirdest. And I didn't mention it because, well, it was weird. But it happened after I got home from school yesterday. To be honest, I was pretty happy coming home. The cop jacket was done and put away. I just had to finish the shoulders on Karl's jacket. On the bus ride home I realized how easy that could be. Why cut and sew the jacket? I could just stuff something in the shoulders and give Karl the size and toughness he totally lacks. There were plenty of scraps to make shoulder pads. I'd just sew them in this afternoon and I'd be all done.

I hopped up the step and opened the door. Mom wasn't in the kitchen, which was definitely not normal. I called "Hello!" but I didn't get an answer. I opened the back door and examined the fridge. The date on the milk was a little off but the carton smelled okay, thanks to our double-cold conditions, so I brought it in and poured a glass. There were seven pretzels left in the bag. I counted out three and put them on my fingers like rings, Tod-style. I know better than to finish the bag.

It's tricky opening a bedroom door with pretzels on my fingers. But it's easier than turning a doorknob with a glass of milk, which always ends badly.

Mom was on my bed. She was wearing her tomato pincushion and a frown. The purple suitcase was open, and the costumes were all over my bed.

Mom was sitting on my costumes. She was manhandling a black jacket. The jacket was inside-out. The silky, gold-colored lining material inside the sleeves was spread out on her lap. A thread was being pulled tight between the jacket and her teeth. This was some major surgery she was doing. She didn't look up.

Mom was holding the Landlord's jacket. My jacket. From my room. From my ugly suitcase. Before I could even put my outrage into words, she totally steamrolled me.

"Come here," she said instead of *hello*.

Uh-oh. The combination of *come here* and no eye contact usually almost always means major trouble.

I stood closer. She held her hand, palm up, right under my nose.

"My measuring tape."

I paused, caught.

"Give it to me."

Like a sheep, I did what she told me, scrunching around my pocket until I came up with the yellow fabric ruler with the metal ends. It was wadded into a ball, which I dropped into her waiting hand.

There was no talking, no chance for me to demand a lock on my door. No sounds at all until she straightened out her precious tape and removed whatever wrinkles she imagined were there. Then she started fussing with the sleeve of the coat, turning it right-side-out again.

I wondered what she was going to do to me.

"Sit down."

I sat.

"These stitches. You can't be serious."

Mom pointed to Luz's measurement list, which she had found in the bag. Then she took the tape and measured the arm from end to end. "I assume you got the length right for this one?"

"Sixteen inches, yeah."

"Close enough. This is butchery. You didn't even cut away the lining. You went *through* the lining. I don't want to see this kind of lazy work again." Those were her *polite* words. After that, she cussed like a sailor while she continued ripping out the stitches I had inflicted on each of the jacket's arms.

"Look," she finally said, calming down. "Mending and alterations are all about return business. You do a good job, you make a living. If you're a butcher, you won't get repeat business. Now watch."

And sure enough, my mom showed me how to shorten a coat sleeve without leaving a trace. She did the first one, and watched me do the other. I know I did a pretty good job because she didn't make me do it over. I could write down what she showed me, but I won't. It's a family secret.

As you can probably guess, I ended up sitting cross-legged like a third grader on my bed with my mother, explaining just about everything that had been going on in school. We took turns surprising the hell out of each other.

"I don't go in your room for anything," she admitted.

"You know that. You keep it clean enough. But I had to look for the drugs."

I nearly stood up. "Drugs? What drugs? I don't even *like* drugs."

She put her hand on my leg and sat me back down. Yeah, she'd figured that out. I had raised her suspicions after spending the four-day weekend cooped up quietly in my room.

"Go figure," she said. "The suburbs are full of moms who go looking for clothes and find their kids hiding drugs. Me? My ghetto juvenile delinquent isn't hiding drugs. He's hiding costumes. He's even *sewing* the costumes. *For the school play!* You could have knocked me over with a feather."

Mom said *school play* the way she usually says *prison.* I couldn't be sure which one she dislikes more.

So I told her all the terrible tales of threads and theater, except for the parts about shopping on clotheslines and my night at the laundromat and raiding Mrs. T.'s dry-cleaning dumpster and anything else that could be held against me. Except for those little details (and anything about the evil sphinx), I told her almost everything, even how Rob bruised my knuckles. The part she liked best was how I got five bucks from the Volvo lady. I wondered if she'd ask me for the money. No, she gave me credit for being clever. And she liked when I showed her the photos in *The Illustrated Immigrant*, where I got my ideas.

In a real warm house, this could have been a real warm moment. But here on my street, I was just happy I wasn't getting punished. I told Mom that I was delivering the costumes to Luz tomorrow.

"Not like this, you're not," she said.

"What?"

"I'm not letting you. Period."

"Nuts to you!" I said, raising my voice, ending our storybook afternoon. "Maybe I didn't do the masterful job you would have done. Luz told me to ask you and I did you a favor and left you out and sewed these myself because I knew you wouldn't help me. So if all my work is ugly butcher garbage, I don't care. I'm getting this out of my hair tomorrow, and you're not going to stop me!"

Mom got steely hard, and right away. She put up both her palms like she was stopping a runaway horse. "Whoa. Calm down, boy. Lower your voice this instant."

I stopped. And she continued.

"You are an absolute idiot, you know that? The rest of your sewing isn't bad. But if you insist on pretending I did this job, then you're getting rid of the God-awful mildew smell. I thought you had a dead body in here. I'm calling in a favor with Mrs. Tagliapietra. She'll dry-clean all this musty junk for free. That hideous bag, too. Pack it up and bring it over now. She'll have it ready in an hour. Now get over there before she closes."

"She can do it in an hour?"

"Have you ever read the sign? It says *One Hour Dry Cleaning*. Guess what that means."

Mom's right. I am an absolute idiot. Just like the guy I inherited it from. I folded the clothes and packed them back into the huge purple bag. Just before I was done, Mom put her hand on mine.

"Oh, one more thing. Leave out this kerchief you stole from my boss. She probably won't recognize the shirt you cut up, but why risk it? I'll wash it here."

Mom snapped the kerchief out of my hand and went into the kitchen. I walked out the front door, stunned. Not stunned because she'd figured out about the stolen red-and-white-striped shirt, or any of the rest of that crazy afternoon. I was stunned that she said my sewing wasn't bad. From her, it was a standing ovation.

Anyway, that was yesterday. Time to go. Study Hall is over.

Tuesday, November 30 (Part 2)

I'm writing this extra-special second installment in English class. It's not even lunchtime yet and I'm writing for the second time today.

They're talking about *Lord of the Flies*. I've read it fourteen times. I live it every day. I can answer any question Harmon can throw at me. But he's not going to ask me anything. Somebody ripped up his writer quotes in the hall today. Left a real mess. He gave me a frustrated, disgusted look when I walked in the room. I can guess what that means.

So I've put on my Stupid Tod face for Harmon. I don't want to be interrupted, either. I'm in too good of a mood. I want to write.

I did it. I delivered the goods. Can you believe it? That's why I came to school late. It's over at last.

I know I wrecked my lifetime perfect attendance record. I'll have to live with the shame. But there was no way I was going through the metal detectors with my jumbo bag of clothes during morning rush when everyone could see me. I get too much attention already. So, I slept a little late, took a different bus, snuck up the walk, and hefted my bag onto the guard's table. She took a look at my stuff and she laughed, swiveling side to side on her torn vinyl chair.

"Moving in?"

"Yeah. I'm going to live in the cafeteria."

"Well, you look like you do already."

"Yeah. Yeah. You do, too." I couldn't think of anything funny.

"How come you're always staring at that crazy race car statue anyway?"

"I dunno. Probably I want to be a sculptor." It never dawned on me she'd notice.

"You won't be a sculptor living in the cafeteria."

"I work with mashed potatoes," I said, looking around.

"I bet you do," she said. "What's all this for? Smells nice."

"These clothes are . . . for the play." I said it like I was lying.

"Yeah, yeah," she said. "Get a late pass at the office."

"Right."

I walked straight toward the auditorium and away from the office. The guard called after me. "I liked that first one better." Whatever that meant.

I ducked down the side hallway, past the nurse's office, around to the backstage door of the auditorium. Nobody saw me, not even the nurse. I wasn't surprised to find Luz climbing down a ladder, waving a hammer and yelling. The set was almost done. I had to admit it looked pretty good. There was a store on one side, with fake stuff painted on the shelves, and a toy cash register on a table. The other side was a school with some chairs. Upstairs on the high part was supposed to be a poor person's home. I recognized it immediately.

Everything was painted on gigantic sheets of hanging canvas, 10 feet high and nearly as wide. One of the sheets had started to come down. That's why Luz had the hammer, I guess. Otherwise she was nearly done painting the old city skyline across the top of the canvas sheets. Now she was on the ground, still yelling. She had black paint on her face and hands, but for once it wasn't on purpose.

"No, no! That's supposed to be a bed. It looks like a chair!"

"It's a bed," said the poor carpenter, who was on loan from Wood Shop and obviously tired of slaving for Luz. He had a hammer, too. Maybe there'd be some action.

"Beds are long. Chairs are short. Do *you* sleep in a chair?" asked Luz, more impatient than I'd ever heard her. "Because I don't. I sleep in a bed. We're running out of time. Make it longer."

A pause.

"Please."

The kid with the bed to build walked away, muttering to

me under his breath. "Bats don't use beds. She sleeps upside down in a cave."

I grunted. Luz noticed me standing on the side of the stage and her eyes shot right to the bag. When she saw the bulge, she smiled.

"MIS-ter Munn!" she cheered. "My hero!"

She was way too loud. Immediately, I stepped back between the extra curtains and the long piece of canvas that the store was painted on. It was dark back there—and it was the closest hiding place to the door. Good for a quick escape. I didn't want her artsy carpenter friends to see me.

"Uh, you'd better hold the excitement until you see what you got."

"Did you give your mom my thank-you note?" she asked as she pulled the bag off my shoulder. "Unh. It's heavy." Luz flicked on a portable workman's light that was hooked to a pipe, so we could finally see back there. Being in the dark with Luz was kind of uncomfortable.

"It's a wardrobe for seven people," I said, sounding bored, like I was reading from a list. "Coats, pants, dresses. A couple of vests, no hats. No shoes. No underwear. I hope your actors can manage with their own underwear."

"Ooh, good," said Luz, holding up the Mother's dress. "Yep, the dad. This is for the Criminal, right? Did your mom do the correct sizes? You gave her the list?"

"She saw the list, yeah. You're not allowed to mention her name. Not on the program. Nowhere."

Luz ignored me. She was a kid at the circus. Her eyes were

on fire, her hands were everywhere, stroking the fabrics, fingering the lapels, testing the seams. She was nodding and murmuring. I was saving the best for last.

"This is the dress for the Teacher?" She held it up to her shoulders—the pink dress with the white circles. Exactly the dress Greg caught me holding up last Wednesday at the Helping Hand, except now the waist was smaller and the collar was changed. Luz stepped out behind the canvas. She held the dress to her own shoulders and spun in a circle, looking at the dress from all sides, up at the light, then back at me. I figured she'd have something to say about the Daughter's dress, not this one. I was getting impatient.

"The Teacher's dress?"

"Yes. Come back in here. You done?"

"Hmmm." She wanted me to believe she was lost in thought. "Okay," she finally said, stepping back into the hideout. After about 50 years, Luz put down the circle-covered dress, and she picked up Karen's dress. The Daughter's.

"This won't work."

"Why not?"

"Karen wants costume control. She is turning into a major pain. I can tell you this dress will make her look like she eats food."

"I'm not . . . getting my mom to make another one."

"No, don't worry. Karen can bring me her own. They've got bucks."

"It won't wreck her acting?"

Luz laughed at me.

"Am I done here?" I insisted.

"Hold on," said Luz. "Nice pocket watch your mom made. I like the vest. Your mom does great work."

I don't know why it bugged me that Mom was getting all the credit.

"I made the watch. The vest belongs to my mom's husband. If you wreck it, I'm dead."

Luz took a piece of chalk from her pocket and made an X inside Dick's vest. "Don't wreck the stepfather's vest. Got it."

Usually I seethe if anyone calls Dick my stepfather. This time I made an exception. To speed things up. After all, I was supposed to be in Science class. I wasn't even signed in yet.

Luz came to the end of the bag. She scratched her head. "Um, where's the policeman's jacket?"

"Over here," I said. I walked her to the place where the graffiti-covered curtain met the graffiti-covered sound controls. I pushed back the curtain and there was my masterpiece, the police uniform, dangling from a hanger on a nail. Right where I left it yesterday. Maybe I'm not in her play, but I know drama.

Luz totally appreciated the extra touch. She reached for the coat. She held it up to the light and gently touched the silver buttons.

"Really, really nice."

"Really?" I asked, before I could catch myself.

"Yeah, very nice Keystone Kop coat. These buttons are great." She gently circled a button with her fingers. "It feels like a bottle cap. Smart. I can see you put the silver foil to good use."

I forgot she'd seen me boost the foil. "Yeah. I did those, too. The buttons and the watch."

She looked at me with a new kind of smile. "I bet you did. How'd you fix the bottle caps to the coat? They're on nice and snug."

"Super-glued paperclips onto the back of the bottle caps. Used an upholstery needle to hook the clips with heavy-gauge thread."

I think I had said too much. Luz took a good look at me, then back at the cop jacket.

"Uh-huh," she said. "Pants fit?"

"If you measured 'em right," I answered quickly, trying to derail her train of thought. I started to feel very nervous. "Look, just keep the vest safe. You can donate the rest. See ya." I took three steps toward the door.

"Wait!" called Luz. "One more thing, okay?"

I never wanted to leave a place as much as I wanted to leave this hot, airless backstage alley with Luz. But I returned to the safe cover of the canvas backdrop. The curse of the sphinx was never going to end. Never, ever.

"What? What do you want from me?"

She put out her fingers to count. It sure looked like more than one thing was coming.

"First, thanks. Really. Thank you. And thank your mom for what she did, okay? And second . . ." She paused for a moment, before speeding up her words.

"Second, you've got to change the Criminal's outfit. Karl Dingle is out. Eric Pomeroy is in." She said this *very* quickly.

"You got rid of Karl Dingle? How come?"

"You told me to fire him. I do listen, ya know. Anyway, he was a pretty big twit. And not very nice."

"How so?"

"Never mind that. Just please change the suit to fit Eric Pomeroy. I've got his measurements here." She handed me a new sheet of paper, covered with her nice handwriting. This time, the paper was a very bright blue. I scanned it quickly.

"Okay," I said, "this'll be easy. He's got the same size pants. Arms are right, but his shoulders are a lot wider. The coat already fits. Just pull the shoulder pads out of the jacket. There aren't many stitches."

I sifted through the bag and picked up the coat, turning it inside out. I took out my house key and used it like a knife to rip out the stitches. From each shoulder popped one half of the padded bra. I told you, I don't like Karl. Let him wear a bra onstage.

Luz got a great laugh out of the bra pads. "Don't need these," she said. She held up the renovated coat and nodded approvingly. "Perfect!" she said.

"We done?"

"Yeah. Thanks a ton, Tod. These are really great. They smell good, too. We've got three days to practice in actual costumes before the play on Friday afternoon."

"Three days," I repeated. "And even better, you got them on November thirtieth."

"Yeah? Why's that better?" she asked.

"To ease your pain from not being Artist of the Month anymore."

"Oh, God, that," she said. "I'm so done with that. I'm glad it's over."

"But it made you world famous."

"I can live without that kind of fame. I was always having to fix the thing, keep it clean. Then a couple of weeks ago, some dweeb totally busted my statue. Probably the janitor. Good thing I had another one at home."

This stopped me cold. Tod vanished. Stupid Tod came stumbling out.

"You have . . . had . . . another sphinx?"

"Yeah. My prototype. I loved making that one. Now I'm making a much bigger one in my garage. *Chops Major*, I'm calling it. It's Styrofoam."

"You had an extra sphinx?" I asked again, squinting my eyes.

"Yep. Lucky me, right?" Then she looked me over. "Why does that bug you?"

"I dunno," I sighed, backing away. "I just thought it was one-of-a-kind or something. Now I'm not so sure about buying it for my collection."

"You can *have* it, okay? Fair trade for the costumes?"

I think I smiled. "Really?"

"Yep. Just take it home today. It's the end of the month. When they arrest you, we'll have a story to tell 'em."

"Well, I mean . . . well, thanks," I said. I decided it would fit on my top shelf, over my bed, to replace the trophy. I could see it there already.

"You can keep the bag. The purple bag," I said.

"Lucky me."

"Thanks."

"Forget it. *Thank you*, Tod. And your mom, I mean. Thanks a lot." Then Luz went back up her ladder, humming something. Two hours later, I'm feeling pretty good. Pretty darn good.

Okay, it's almost the end of class. Mr. Harmon didn't call on me once. Now I'm certain he thinks I ripped up his doorway. Let him. Let him deal with Stupid Tod. I don't care.

★ ★ ★ Now Mrs. Woodrow, here's a special note for you.

It's the last day of the month. You told me I could be done with this detention "in about a month." Okay, it's been, like, six weeks. November is up. With all due respect, if you don't mind, I'd very much like to suggest that this afternoon be what we could call the "last day" of detention. Everything is working out pretty well. And as much as I love hanging out here with you, I'd be very happy to go back to my usual afternoons of leisure and social responsibility.

Have I learned my lesson? Yes. Will I do anything so foolish again to myself, my reputation, and my school? Gosh, no. Never. Never, ever. Will I let myself be misled by the treachery of others? I swear on my life that I will not. Am I telling you the truth?

Why not?

Will you at least think about it, please, Mrs. W.? Nothing

personal, but my arm is really tired of writing. I'll admit that sitting with you each day has definitely been better than gathering candy wrappers in the snow, no fooling. I appreciate that.

There's the bell. Can you believe how much writing I did? And it's only Tuesday. I'm going to drop off the notebook to you on the way to lunch. Please read it before detention this afternoon. I'll put a note at the top of all the writing I did today so you'll read this.

I've enjoyed this buddy movie of ours. It's been fun.

Monday, December 6

Dear Tod,

Last week was a truly unforgettable week. Here is the part where you fulfill your last obligation to me before your detention is over for good.

As we agreed, please take the pages you wrote last week in your private notebook and staple them into this detention notebook. I would also appreciate your adding a few paragraphs explaining how you came to start writing in your other notebook, and what happened after you got suspended.

Thank you again, Tod.

—Judith Woodrow

Ugh. Okay. Fine. I don't want to do this. I'm only doing this for you. If it gets me off the hook, fine. Whatever it takes. But it's sure going to be more than a few paragraphs.

I guess this all started when you came to my house.

To tell you the truth, I was pretty surprised to find you at my front door last Thursday evening. It was a lot more surprising than me getting suspended from school on Tuesday. That's for sure.

Just think. I got suspended after school on the last day of November. I had almost made it through the whole, short month of November without getting suspended.

I didn't care. Really didn't care about a month's vacation. What was I going to miss if I didn't come back until January? Yearbook photos? The stupid play? Exams? Even if I got shut out of every test, my grades are plenty good to carry me through a failed midterm. Too bad. You wouldn't get to flunk me out.

No, I didn't mean you personally, Mrs. W. . . . I meant your school.

Anyway, what were the words my mom used? Knock me over with a feather? That's what you did by showing up last Thursday night. But that wasn't nearly the weirdest part.

You can probably guess that we don't get a lot of teachers here in our neighborhood. Certainly not in my house. I'd already heard two days of dire warnings and threats from my mom about my actions. I'll say she had me pretty convinced that Carnegie wouldn't let me come back to school, not in January or ever. It looked like you had washed your hands of me.

Maybe even you personally, Mrs. W.

I couldn't read your face at the suspension meeting on

Tuesday after school. You didn't say a word, really. But there you were, two days later, knocking on our door in your solid black shoes and your long blue woolly winter coat and your dark yellow scarf with the gray curls popping out and your bulletproof gray purse on its fat chain. Trust me, that purse would make a really good weapon if you needed one.

From my room I saw you come up the walk, stepping over the tree roots and the garbage bags. I'm sure you saw me in there reading, but you acted like you couldn't see into my fishbowl. Thanks for the privacy, I guess. For your information, the next day was garbage day. That's why I put the garbage bags out. It's not like there's always garbage in front of our house.

Well, I sure wasn't going to be the person who answered the door. I intended to sit in my room until long after you left. You probably didn't want to see your failed experiment in his natural habitat. I figured you came by to get Mom to sign whatever papers would release me immediately into the criminal justice system.

Having you and Mom in the same living room could have been interesting. I was expecting Mom to go one of two ways—either yell you out the door or freeze you out until you retreated. I never would have guessed that you'd all end up in an actual, respectable conversation. Thanks to my hollow door, I could hear a little of what you guys were talking about on the couch. Even Dick had things to say. When I heard him laugh a couple of times, I thought I was in the wrong house. Then it came.

"Tod! Will you please come out here?"

You have no idea how weird it is to lay on my bed and hear my guidance counselor call me into my living room. What could I do? With my mom, I've got a complete arsenal of clever replies. With you, I was unarmed. Stalling wouldn't have worked, either. You were six feet from my door, perfectly positioned between me and the bathroom. I didn't have a chance. So, I turned the knob.

There you were, all of you, side by side. The three people who had the most control over my life, my liberty, and my pursuit of happiness. Nobody looked mad. Also, none of you seemed to know who was leading the conversation. My folks looked at you, Mrs. W., so you took the lead. And you blew me away with your unexpected greeting.

"Good evening, Tod. Have you been keeping a journal here at home since your suspension two days ago?"

Huh? How did you know? How?? Were you watching me through my front window? Did my mom search my room when I was bagging the garbage? I heard you talking to Mom about my school detention notebook, but there is NO WAY you could have known what else I was up to. I don't believe in lucky guesses. I decided—absolutely—that I would keep the existence of my private, at-home notebook absolutely, totally private.

"Yeah," I mumbled. "I have. I've kept a notebook."

That's when you and my mother exchanged glances. You crossed your hands over your lap and looked me straight in the eye.

"Would you get it for me, Tod? Please?"

I don't know why, but I put my arms up against the sides of my doorway. It probably looked like I was barricading my room against an attack. But I was only making sure I wouldn't fall over.

Mom didn't wait for you to ask me a second time. She took her best shot.

"Please, buddy. Get it now."

It was the combination of "*please*" and "*buddy*" from Mom that disarmed me completely. She and my father used to call me *buddy* all the time, until maybe second grade, when *poof*! He was gone and I made sure I wasn't anyone's buddy anymore. Sometimes Mom leaks out a "buddy" when she's scared or worried about me, but that's pretty rare nowadays.

Without another thought, I went back into my room and shoved a hand under my mattress. Out came the yellow notebook with the yellow pages. Up above, James Bond shot me a dirty look from behind his pistol. I couldn't bear to look at him at all. Some secret agent I turned out to be. Without a struggle, without a fuss, I totally cracked. I handed over my most sacred and private possession to my detention warden in under thirty seconds.

And here it is, stapled right where you wanted it.

Wednesday, December 1

Hey there, yellow pad.

Got busted yesterday. Big time. I'm pretty much going to be hiding in my room for the next month. I'd rather watch TV in here, but my room doesn't have cable or a satellite hookup or a TV. My computer is still in the store, and so is my stereo. My little music player is out of batteries. I have decided to wait for the best and newest phone to come out. Until then, I can't make calls. The newspaper and magazine subscriptions have all expired. My public library card is being held hostage to $37 in overdue fees. Totally unfair. My expert knowledge of smoke signals and Morse code won't help me order a pizza. I don't have any money for stamps. Or anyone to write to. So I'm stuck here with you. Good thing you're a jumbo! With 300 pages! College ruled! And most of your yellow pages are still blank. December is going to suck.

I'm not totally without something new to read. Yesterday I was handed a brochure in the office waiting area that's a total hoot. It's called *Anger Management for the Angry Teenager.* I didn't have anything else to read yesterday afternoon, waiting for my mom to abandon her work and haul over to school to hear what a deviant I am. I wasn't on either end of that call, but I can only imagine what choice words she had with Evil Prince Ipple. And the other way around, I'm sure.

Table of Contents
What is anger?
What are the causes of teen anger?
What are the symptoms of teen anger?
What is within the teen's control?
What is out of the teen's control?
What can change at home?
What can change at school?
What can the concerned adult do?

I can't tell what's funnier to me—that the brochure says it's about anger management for *angry* teenagers, instead of happy ones, or that the brochure isn't any bigger than a piece of folded notebook paper. I guess if I'd read this brilliant skinny little booklet months ago, I'd be all cinnamon and roses, dozing off in Math class right now instead of on my bed. No, wait. School's over. I'd be writing my arm off in detention. Now *that's* funny.

Hey! No more detention for me!

What are the causes of teen anger? How about being ambushed by your so-called friends in the cafeteria? That would do it.

I was in a really great mood after I handed off the clothes to Luz. I'm sorry I didn't get to send Karl on stage with a padded bra. But I felt pretty slick adjusting the Landlord's shoulders right on the spot! I wondered if Luz suspected how involved I was in the costumes. Nah.

Then I did all that writing in Study Hall and English. I'm

getting really fast. And six weeks later, I don't even realize I'm writing anymore. It just happens. I look up and an hour's gone by, and everything I've been thinking about is right there on the paper. It's interesting how much thinking I end up doing when I write. I remember things pretty well, too. Back at the start of detention, Mrs W. made me promise that I wouldn't make up anything, and I kept my word the whole time. I just left stuff out if it could get someone in trouble. (Like me.) Sometimes for fun I dropped little hints.

Anyway, Tuesday, November 30, was one of the best days of my life. Until lunchtime. Then, without a moment's warning, it became one of the worst.

I dropped off my detention notebook in Mrs. W.'s office before heading into the lunchroom. Since I came late to school yesterday to give Luz the costumes, I'd missed free hot breakfast, so I was pretty hungry. I was hoping Bernie would be in the lunchroom so we could all just have a nice, normal game of cards. I turned the corner into the cafeteria and *bang!* I walked right into Rex and Rob, leaning against the wall. They were waiting for me. Ambush.

"Ooh, delivery boy, brought a big present for your sweetie?" cooed Rob.

"What is *with* you guys?" I demanded. "Where have you been? What are you talking about?"

Rex took a drag on the toothpick in his mouth and pretended to exhale. "We're waiting here 'cause of you, Pops," he said evenly. No emotion. He was leaning on the wall like he was holding it up. I couldn't read him at all. But I wasn't going to start something. I needed Rex to help get Rob back in line.

Rob chimed in and smiled at Rex. "Yeah, Pops."

"I saw you out the window during Auto Shop," said Rex. "You were coming up the walk with your cute purple body bag."

I wasn't liking the tone of this. Unfortunately, I didn't have an answer. Time to stall. "Do you have any idea what you're even talking about?"

"Yeah, Pops," said Rex. "I know exactly what I'm talking about. Let's take a walk."

Now, normally, it's me doing the pushing and some sucker getting pushed. But this time, Rex was being the heavy and I couldn't exactly figure out why. The math was simple. If I didn't listen to Rex, he could go ape right there in the cafeteria.

I remember thinking, He's not afraid of getting suspended, but I do NOT want a phone call going out to my mom. Not today. I want my detention to end. End of the month. Today.

So we walked.

We walked side by side down the main hall, me in the middle. We walked past the auditorium and the sounds of people rehearsing the play. We walked past the voice of Luz yelling an excited *yes!*

Rex and Rob and I walked out the front door, just like old friends. Except.

The guard lady ignored us, reading her magazine. We went through the front door, and I took a look up at my new sphinx as I passed it. I decided I wouldn't call it Mr. Chops. Rex saw me turn my neck to the statue and he gave a snort. We stopped just outside the front door. Nobody could hear us talk.

I found myself with my back to the wall and my two dear friends facing me. I tried to get back the upper hand. "Rob's got some explaining to do. My hand still hurts from his racket attack. He's lucky we're still friends."

"Friends?" started Rob, but Rex gave him a look. The General was going to take over.

"Listen, Pops. Things aren't so good lately," said Rex, sounding a lot older all of a sudden. "Lot of bad blood. First it's you relaxing in the tower while we're freezing in the trash pile every afternoon. Then it's—"

"Wait a minute," I interrupted, talking fast. "You're the reason we got *caught* that night, Rex. You and your out-of-control vandal wreckage. We would have gotten out clean. Way I see it, I'm stuck in detention because of *you*."

Rex just shook his head. "You were the man with the plan, Pops. You led, we followed. I maybe lost my temper, but that wasn't my fault. There wasn't any camera to steal. We'd already set off the alarm. You didn't do enough planning, that's what. You let your revenge get in the way."

"Wrong, Einstein. *We* didn't set off the alarm. *You* did, when we found Greg's IOU instead of the video camera. You're the one who decided to knock over the TV cart and swing a chair leg through the window. *That's* where the alarm is. On the windows."

Rex turned stiff. "You pushed that chair into the window . . ."

I turned stiffer. "I was stopping you. From smashing the TV."

After the 200th time, this argument wasn't ever going to change. Rob knew it, and that's why he felt brave enough to jump in.

"All for one and one for all, right, Pops? Rex and me had plenty of time spiking trash to talk over your sweet deal with Mrs. Woodrow. You think you're going to sell your story, Pops? Think anyone wants to read the sad story of a poor, fat loser?"

Rob knows that my patience runs thin when he's calling me a loser. Now it was even thinner than the time I poked a badminton racket into his scrawny chest. Standing behind Rex, who fights like a cougar, Rob seemed to be feeling pretty brave.

I took a deep breath and shifted my weight from my gut to my chest. "Shut up, okay, Rob?" I said. "I get your point. You're unhappy. Now let the grown-ups talk. What are you after, Rex?"

"Just this, Pops. We put up with a lot. You got the cushy detention, you got the good grades, you were the leader, Pops. You got it all. Then guess what? You dumped us for that freak-a-zoid goth girl. She's got you chit-chatting in lunch, running errands, lugging luggage, dancing onstage with the losers. She's got you embarrassing yourself in a dress. A *dress*!"

"Everyone's laughing at you, you know," Rob added, eagerly.

"Shut UP, Rob!" I threatened.

"We don't see you for days," continued Rex. "You act all crazy. You act all important. Too important for your loser pals."

He was talking so much crap I didn't know where to begin. At this point, only one thing mattered.

"And what about Bernie? He joining your new girls' club, too?"

Rob pitched in. "You can forget about Bernie."

"What's that supposed to mean, huh?"

"It means he's a goner," said Rex. "He ain't coming back."

My fists curled up tight. "What'd you do to Bernie?"

Rex just flicked his toothpick at me. It bounced off my cheek. I reached back my arm to crush my fist against his demented hillbilly head when Mrs. Parker, the world's oldest teacher, came out the door. She gave us a sour face.

"Boys? Back to the cafeteria. Now, please."

Rob giggled. I swear he did. Giggled and said, "Okay, Mrs. Parker." Rob went in first, with Rex right behind. Once he was in the entryway, Rex turned around to face me.

"You traded us in for a girl, Toddy Bear. And an ugly one, too. We won't forget it." Then he kicked the pedestal with the sphinx and disappeared around the corner.

"Hey!" yelled the guard.

I ran over to catch the statue in case it fell. It wobbled and shifted, but it didn't come down. I reached up and tried to put things right. But that's getting harder and harder all the time. After school, that baby was mine.

Okay. That was my relaxing lunch. The bell was about to ring and I hadn't eaten anything. I headed upstairs to my locker, where I was saving a vending machine cupcake. A triangle of paper was sticking out of the air slits. It was too small to pick through the outside of the door. While I turned the combination lock, my mind wandered. This could be another note from Luz. The kind of note that couldn't be taped to the outside of a guy's locker. The door swung open.

The note wasn't from Luz. It was ripped from a homework sheet—the last paper I wrote for Bernie. And it had a bloody thumbprint on it. A real one.

D+S are crazy their going to FD
today and rex plays art

Oh, no. I swiveled my head left and right fast. Nobody was watching. Nobody was in the hall. I balled up Bernie's note and jammed it in my pocket. I hopped down the stairs two at a time. Major hurry. And right when I hit the bottom step, the bell rang. Doors opened and the hall filled with clueless students and bumbling teachers blocking my way. I dodged, I bumped, I knocked a few down by mistake, maybe. I felt like I was on the wrong end of a meteor storm. Then I passed a couple of blind kids and had to slow down. By the time I got near the lunchroom, another flood of kids was stumbling out like recently fed cows. For extra slowness, the janitor had his stepladder out to change a lightbulb.

Detour. I opened one of the doors of the office and walked past the long row of teacher cubbyhole mailboxes. Past the time clock. Past the water cooler. And out through the other door. If I raised any eyebrows, I didn't have time to notice. I crossed to the auditorium and ducked around the side hall. The nurse's door was closed. Further down, around the corner, the stage door was closed and locked. But it's one of those double doors that isn't too secure. A strong jerk could get it open. And I was just the jerk to do it.

I closed the door behind me. No one was on the stage or in the auditorium, best as I could tell. I thought about going up on the catwalk for a better view. But I couldn't jump down when the time came, not like James Bond would. So I slipped behind the fake canvas store and curled up in the dark. I kept my eyes on the door. And I fell asleep.

When I woke up, I was seriously hungry. There was no way to know what time it was. If I could have seen it, my watch from the Helping Hand would have said 6:30. It *always* says 6:30—both of its helpless hands dangle like pendulums.

The play was in full rehearsal. Dress rehearsal. Luz had finagled permission to pull the actors from afternoon classes on the last few days before the show. Kids were talking over each other. Luz was talking over the kids. Someone was hammering. Someone dropped a bunch of coins, or maybe nails. Someone was whispering close to me. A girl.

"It's hideous. Even Luz wouldn't wear that rag." Was it Karen?

A boy giggled quietly and whispered. "And that's saying something."

The girl went *tsk* with her tongue. "I called my mom. She hates that she has to get me a new dress. I thought this play would do something for me. What a joke. I'd drop out just to mess Luz up, except my name's on the poster. I'm fourth from the top! It's not even alphabetical!" Now I knew it was Karen talking.

"Friday is just three more days," said the boy. It wasn't the boy playing the Father. Not the boy playing the Cop. He's way too ugly to be Karen's friend. Not the Landlord either. Someone else. The new crook? A stage helper?

"At least you're on the poster," he added. Okay, this was Eric Pomeroy. Luz's new criminal genius. Karl's replacement.

"It would be nice if you gave me flowers after the play."

"Aw, c'mon, Karen. I can't keep stealing from my folks. I just paid you. They're gonna notice."

Karen's voice suddenly went cold. Stone cold. "You don't bring me flowers, you better pay me another ten dollars," she said. My ears went on big-time alert. Here's what I heard:

"I got Karl kicked off the play for not paying enough. I got you his part in the play. You want what happened to Rashawn and Ricardo and Jeremy Gibson to happen to you?"

"Don't break my phone. Keep him away from my phone."

"He will kick your butt," growled Karen. Really growled.

"Ten dollars? And that's it for the rest of the year? You promise?"

"Don't push it. I want it tomorrow. And remember, if the Munnster finds out, you're dead."

I didn't hear the rest. I didn't have to. I got enough.

While I stewed in my hot dark hideout, I pieced it all together. How stupid was I? Ricardo and Rashawn and Jeremy had been my best-paying rich-kid customers. They're the punks who go out of their way to make you feel bad 'cause they've got a new video game or mountain bike and you don't. Since last spring, these kittens had been more than happy to pay me a buck or two to leave them alone for a week. I never had to do a thing, just push them a little, stand close, keep up the tough-guy act.

Then in October it all dried up. They stopped lending me their candy money at about the same time. Finally I lost it with Ricardo. I made a stupid threat, and I had to follow through. He just lay down and took it. When he found out I got sent home, he told Carnegie it was an accident. He even told me his insurance would pay for the glasses. Like he was apologizing. It made no sense.

Now the answer fell into my lap. Karen Dominick muscled me out of my turf. Curvy Karen? Seriously? Why? She's cute, she smells great, she's got more money than most of them, I'm pretty sure. She hangs out with Greg and his Vidiots. She doesn't need . . . Greg? Greg is her enforcer? Nah. Impossible. Whoever it is, busting a kid's phone is major. Bigger than glasses. Broken phones really piss off the parents. And you might not get another one.

This wasn't about money. It was about power. And being mean. I'm just a guy trying to make a few bucks. She's really stinking mean. In fact, she's so mean she couldn't even be bothered to start her own customer list. She had to go for mine. Somebody was watching me, took names, and took over. It had to be one of the jackals in the video club.

Greg's probably the mastermind of all this. He's had it in for me since way before the spelling bee. Because my grades are always better than his. He even said so. I know that's why he puts those stupid videos of me on the Internet. *Todd's Odds*, he calls them. Doesn't even spell my name right.

Sometimes in the library I go check out the videos when I'm alone. They're each about a minute long. They get hundreds of hits. Hundreds. Why do hundreds of people want to see me picking my nose, scratching my arms, or making that face with my tongue when I'm reading? With that stupid music. The Vidiots aren't even subtle. They play games trying to hide the camera in a backpack or a box or something. Always around, like mosquitoes. Every time I see them, I'm looking for the camera. Lately they haven't even bothered to hide it.

The comments kids leave on the web site are even more stupid. They're full of spelling mistakes. Greg knows all about those. The only person who ever defended me was Stuart, and he can't even see the videos. Greg's Laugh at Tod Show is definitely illegal. And I know Harmon knows about it. When I mentioned it that day in class, he just about admitted it. Harmon lets them take the video camera out of school. I saw Greg with it on the street a couple of times. Probably at the Helping Hand, too. Then there was his IOU note the night of the break-in.

"Mr. Harmon, I have the camera again for the weekend. Mum's the word! Greg"

Munn's the word, he meant. That piece of paper is my only souvenir from that miserable night. I don't know why I took it. Everyone thought I actually stole the stupid camera until Greg made it magically reappear the next day. He had no idea the trouble he caused. You'd think after everything he's done, I would have shown someone the note to save myself. But why should I narc? Why should I break my own rules? Just to bust Greg? He isn't worth it.

Rex was right—stealing the camera after the spelling bee was supposed to be my revenge against Greg and even Harmon for letting them get away with all this.

It's not fair. Everyone knows about it and nobody ever does anything.

I thought the two episodes of *Todd's Odds* would be enough. But stupid Greg saw me from the tennis team's runty yellow after-school bus. Then he went home and got his brother to drive him back to the Helping Hand Thrift Shop so they could get the one with me and the dress. He had that one posted the next day—220 hits by Monday. And that was over Thanksgiving weekend.

Every one of the stupid comments got it wrong. I don't care if people think I was wearing a dress. No, I got caught sifting through thrift-shop boxes. That's what makes me want to lie down under my porch and never come out.

And I didn't even take a shirt for myself.

So Harmon doesn't like me after all. Big deal. I should have figured the spelling bee was rigged when I heard him apologize to Cornell about me showing up. But keeping me in the dark didn't work, so they let Greg sneak through with *jewellery* spelled the British way. That's why I spelled my word *licence*. Just to see what hypocrites they are. Well, they didn't disappoint me. I know how to spell *license*. After all, I've been staring at my prized, imported-from-London James Bond poster, *Licence to Kill*, ever since I got it from Rob. I guess it's only okay to use British spellings if your family came over on the *Mayflower*.

Harmon's got no spine. His boss made him sneak those green spelling sheets under my nose so I wouldn't wreck their TV show. He didn't stand up to her. He doesn't stand up to Greg, either. He lets his precious vidiots run wild because it's one big privileged club. And when I told Harmon what I knew, he couldn't look me in the eye. No wonder he hates me now. The moron who trashed Harmon's writer quotes saved me the effort. He did me a favor.

Another thing. I know exactly why Luz fired Karl. Not because Karen had any pull. It's because Karl was making Mrs. Munn jokes about the dress video. I'm sure of it.

Wow, this is a lot of writing when I'm not being timed in school. I guess I'm not in such a hurry, am I? I bet the warden would give me another pad when this one is filled. But I'm not taking any chances. I'm writing on both sides of the yellow paper.

Thursday, December 2

I had to do a ton of raking and weeding this morning for one of Dick's customers. I should have seen it coming. School's not looking so bad after all. My whole body is ruined. At least Dick let me go home for lunch. I'm writing instead.

Time to get to the big part.

Back on Tuesday, two long days ago, I had been hiding backstage for about three hours, sweating and sleeping and starving and learning what a snake Karen Dominick is. I know it was three hours because the final school bell rang and I'd been there since the end of lunch. Luz had one more dress rehearsal planned for after school. She was getting pretty anxious. A lot of the kids were getting their lines wrong. And something called blocking. That was wrong too.

I was beginning to question the note I got. I know Bernie was serious. I'm sure he wrote it with a bloody nose, courtesy of Rex. But maybe the plan got called off. Maybe it was going to be tomorrow. This was garbage-picking time. Still, I didn't dare head up to Mrs. Woodrow's. What if I missed the moment? What if I messed up?

If it wasn't Tuesday, I'd have to spend Wednesday huddling and hiding in the dark all over again. Until whenever it happened. Now I know how Stuart feels.

I thought about Mrs. Woodrow getting mad that I had ditched detention. Then I remembered how much writing I'd already done. Maybe that would count in my favor.

While I was still thinking about that, I got lucky. Or I guess that's what you'd call it. About ten minutes after school let out, a never-ending headache of loud bells started going off. Fire drill! Just as Bernie said. Some of the kids were annoyed by the interruption, and the rest were happy to have a break. Luz thought out loud about ignoring the drill. It didn't matter. The actors were already covering their ears and walking past me out the door, looking great in my superb costumes! They were saying the play wasn't worth being burned to death.

My heart pounded—the FD at last. I alone knew what was set to happen. I stood up in the cave between the curtains and the canvas and shook out my stiff legs. My droogs didn't disappoint me.

"Hurry up!"

"Shhhh."

Rex poked his head through the open backstage door. The head looked straight ahead, but the eyes moved left and right. Just the way you're supposed to when you're trying to look innocent and see if the coast is clear at the same time. Rex was good, but only a true master criminal would have suspected me lurking in the shadows, ten feet away. Rex wore his father's ugly hunting coat. He walked a few steps past the door and, certain that the coast was clear, he silently signaled for Rob to follow.

Rob came in, just about on tiptoe. He looked scared to death, with his nice winter parka zipped up high and his hands jammed deep in his pockets.

Rex motioned with his hands to tell Rob to close the

door. He made the same gesture three times, but Rob was clueless. Finally, Rex rolled his eyes, stepped past Rob toward the door, and closed it himself. Then Rex threw some scraps of paper on the floor.

Rob just stood there by the door, looking like a shell-shocked Eskimo whose igloo has just melted.

Rex walked out of view, across the stage about halfway, judging from the sound of his footsteps. If I had moved back farther behind the canvas sheets, I could have peeked between the seams. But the dangling canvas might have fluttered. It would have been too risky, even with the bells going off. I didn't want to make my move until I caught them in the act.

Rob stayed rooted in front of me. He followed Rex with his eyes but not his body. Then Rob nodded and pulled his hands out of his pockets. The idiot was wearing his winter gloves. Something shiny was in his left hand—it caught the light with a flash. It was Bernie's lighter. Rob shook his head "no" at Rex and frantically gestured for Rex to come back. Come back away from the middle of the stage. Come back into the shadows, where cowards and fools can be found. And Rex came back.

They both knelt near me on the other side of the painted canvas. I could see their shadows on the cloth. One of them picked up a corner of the canvas. So this was how they were going to wreck the play's art.

Or, as Bernie put it, *rex plays art*.

"Torch it. Now," said Rex.

"What?" said Rob. The fire-drill bell was still making a lot of noise.

"Now," repeated Rex.

"Why me?" whined Rob.

"Because you've got the gloves, ninny."

There it was: my gang in a nutshell. Smart enough to set up Bernie with his fingerprints on the lighter. Stupid enough to try to light a lighter in winter gloves. It was time.

Oh, right. I didn't have a plan. Three hours hiding and no plan. Figures. So I just punched my hand into the canvas. Rob howled in pain and fell flat.

"What was that?" said Rex.

"Something fell," moaned Rob. I could see his legs twitching from side to side.

Rex leaned up closer against the canvas to see what had happened. I could tell from his shadow that he was peeking through the window. The fake, painted window. This was too good. I landed another direct hit.

"Lord almighty!" yelped Rex, stumbling backward.

Rex isn't the sort of person to lie down when he's been hit. He's the sort who comes around backstage holding a cash register for a weapon.

"Munn!"

"So, we meet at last," I said.

I couldn't resist.

"You're done for!" snapped Rex. Or something like that. He took a swing at me with the register, and I deflected it with my arm. It really hurt. But I had the benefit of surprise, and an accomplice: Rob and his legs. I shoved Rex back and he fell right over Rob. He sprawled over his girlfriend and I jumped on Rex's chest, planning to loosen a few more of his teeth. Rex's shoulders were pinned under my knees, but he grabbed at the canvas and pulled it hard enough to rip it free, fake window and all. All ten feet of canvas came fluttering down on top of us. I held them both down with my extra tonnage. We were one big covered lump, tan on the outside, raging red hot on the inside.

I'm not happy that I was beating up Rex. I had to. At least I couldn't see what I was doing. I had all the advantages. Maybe it's because my eyes were already used to the dark. Maybe hunger had made me crazy. Maybe I was just fed up. Doesn't matter. This was what it was. The finale.

According to Luz, we looked like a bagful of bulldogs, with Rob's legs the only human part sticking out. That's how she found us when she came back into the auditorium.

"MY SET!" she screamed. That's how I knew she was back.

"WHAT ARE YOU DOING? WHO ARE YOU?" she said, all the while hitting me with something. Turned out it was a candlestick. Another prop. All those props really hurt.

"Luz!" I cried. "CUT IT OUT!"

She stopped.

"Tod? What the hell is this?"

"Get a sentry. Get the guard!"

Luz barked the same order to somebody and, inside a minute, arms were pulling the canvas off my pathetic gang.

"Careful! We need that canvas! We don't have time to paint another one!"

"I've got you," said George the Not Famous Ex-Wrestler Sentry. "Come out of there."

Suddenly I was in the light. And it was very bright. Before I had a chance to do anything fun, like focus my eyes or breathe, I found my hands pinned behind me and locked in plastic restraints. George was good at his job.

"Get up," he snarled at me. Snarled, but still sounded bored.

For the record, getting pulled up by your handcuffed wrists while your arms are stretched straight behind your back is a lot more painful than getting punched. Getting punched is a dull feeling. It goes to the muscles. Getting your arms nearly torn out of their sockets attacks the nerves. Muscles take a message and call your brain in the morning. Nerves get your immediate attention.

I stood up *fast*. I didn't look at Rex at all. I didn't have to. I kept my head lowered.

I didn't look at Luz either. With the fire alarm finally quiet, Luz was now providing the soundtrack.

"You horrible . . . ! You bunch of horrible . . . ! Watch that canvas, don't bend it! No! The paint will crack! You miserable . . . ! Why did you do this?! Careful! You miserable, rotten . . . !"

And then the worst part.

"If you even touch that statue, I'll have you arrested."

As I was being led away, I noticed a scrap of paper Rex had tossed to the ground. A cartoon balloon with the word

Twain peered up at me. It was one of Mr. Harmon's quotes. I told you Rex was smart. He was setting me up along with Bernie.

The rest I don't really care to remember. A smug principal, a silent guidance counselor, a proud ex-wrestler, a steaming mother. A mandatory 30-day suspension for fighting. And a stupid brochure about anger management.

What is anger?
It's what happens when good intentions go bad.

What are the causes of teen anger?
See above.

What are the symptoms of teen anger?
Anger.

What is within the teen's control?
Nothing.

What is out of the teen's control?
The teen.

What can change at home?
The locks on the door.

What can change at school?
The right to attend.

What can the concerned adult do?

Be patient until the teen is old enough to be tried as an adult.

Everyone knows that teenagers are unpredictable.

We're variable.

N is a variable.

N + Teenager = Teen anger.

Simple as that.

Monday, December 6 (part 2)

Dear Mrs. W. This is for you.

You see? I stapled the yellow pages into my notebook, just as I promised. Fine. There they are. Now you want me to write about what else happened last week. You've got me writing in my detention notebook *after* my detention is over? Gee, you're good at your job.

I guess I should go back to last Thursday night. As soon as I handed you my yellow notebook, I felt weird. I felt lost. You said, "Thank you, Tod." I said nothing.

While you thumbed through my personal book, I sat down on the coat chair, just staring. My hands were on my knees, and my butt was crushing a two-foot pile of coats. Yours was on top. I was keeping it warm.

As soon as you started reading, Mom and Dick got up and

walked into the kitchen instead of trying to read over your shoulder. That surprised me. I wouldn't have guessed they would have been so considerate. On the other hand, I never would have guessed any of the things that were happening in my house that night.

I guess you've gotten used to reading my scrawl by now, because you went through it all pretty quickly. I was worried you were missing some of the best parts. Not taking enough time to appreciate my technique. After you were done reading, you closed the book and thanked me and asked me a handful of questions.

"Tod, is everything in this journal true?"

"Why would I lie in my private notebook? Doesn't that defeat the purpose?"

"Is it all true, Tod?"

"Yes."

"Did you write all of this after your suspension?"

"Each page has a date on top."

"Thank you," you said, putting the notebook in your iron handbag. "I have to take this with me."

Now things had become officially insane. "Take it? Why? What do you want it for?"

"Tod, I believe you have just provided the proof I need to explain your actions and reverse your suspension. You've also given me other insights that can help me sort out a lot of what's been going on in school lately."

My back went up. "So, you're going to narc on my droogs using this . . . this . . . testimony?"

"Ever loyal, hmm? From what I can tell, they're hardly

your droogs anymore. We have the lighter, but not even your writing would be enough to prove the intent of arson. Their fighting suspensions will have to suffice. I've got other fish to fry. I think you know what I mean."

"You mean Greg."

"Certainly. And his unsanctioned use of the school's video equipment. You tried to take it out of the school and failed. Greg has succeeded. Multiple times. Since your fiasco, we've installed a closed-circuit camera to watch the A/V equipment. Tomorrow we'll check the tape. I expect there will be a new video starring Greg, and he won't like it one bit. But to my eyes, the worst offender is Karen. Imagine a privileged child like her, extorting money for sport. It's disgusting. You've been no better, but your crimes are in the past and hers are in the present. You've also paid a penalty. I'm more inclined to weigh the mitigating circumstances in your case."

"No, Mrs. Woodrow. Don't. I really don't like you using me as a tool to bust other kids. No matter how much they deserve it."

"This isn't the Supreme Court, Tod. But even if it were, remember that you've already handed me your notebook voluntarily. I received the intelligence fair and square. And I intend to present copies of it to the Disciplinary Committee after I've had a talk with everyone involved. Especially Karen's victims."

"Even Mr. Harmon?"

"If he's complicit in this horrible mistreatment of you, yes."

I sighed.

"Tod, there's one thing I still don't understand. Why do you and your former droogs all call each other by nicknames? That wasn't just for the detention notebook. I've heard you all talk. I think I understand Scott's nickname. It comes from his shoplifting hobby. Is that right? He's not very good at it, you know."

I sighed again. This was giving away everything. As if I hadn't already. What the hell.

"I started calling him *Rob* after he got arrested twice in the same week."

"And Donny? Is he called *Rex* because he's a king?"

"Hardly. I doubt he even knows what it means. No, he wrecks anything. And I've been calling Doug *Bernie* since he started torching leaf piles in third grade."

Then I quickly added, "But I'm the one who put an end to that. I keep him under control. Fire is stupid. He knows I'll give him a pop if he messes up, like that morning we went to the dry cleaner's."

You smiled here. "A pop. That's why you're called *Pops*."

"Yeah, I used to pop anyone. The name doesn't really fit me anymore. Except Tuesday with Rex. I didn't even hit Rob with the badminton racket when I could have."

"If you had, I wouldn't be here. Scott was unarmed on the floor of the gym, I recall."

"I guess so."

That's when you stood up and pretended to stretch your neck so you could sneak a look around before you went. We talked a little more. And I finally got up off your coat and let you have it back. You called "*Thank you!*" across the house to Mom and Dick. Mom came out front and thanked you back. She can be very polite when she wants to be. Dick waved from the kitchen table. I opened the front door for you. And just before you left, you asked me for one more thing.

"Tod, there's just one more thing . . ."

I apologize for rolling my eyes right then. But you have to give me some credit. It had been a tough couple of days.

"Yeah?"

"Will you please come to the play tomorrow afternoon? I give you my full permission. I'm not sure if your suspension will be revoked by then, but I'll try. Please come."

I squinted. "Why?"

"You worked hard, Tod. You deserve to see it."

"Luz will kill me."

"I intend to talk with her."

"Maybe."

"And one more thing."

"*Another* one more thing?"

"Will you please write all this down? Including tonight? Put it in your journal?"

"It's a notebook."

"Of course it is. Will you?"

"I wasn't going to."

"Please, Tod?"

"Why?"

"I want to read it, that's why. I was an English teacher for twenty-two years before I became a guidance counselor. Believe me. You're a good writer."

I thought, Wow! Really?

But I said, "No."

"Tod?"

"Sorry, I can't."

"Why not?"

Joke's on you. "Because you're taking my notebook."

So you reached into your armored purse and you pulled out my detention notebook.

"Use this one."

Joke's on me.

Tuesday, December 7

When I walked into school last Friday, I hadn't been there for two whole days. It sure looked the same.

I didn't even know if I was still suspended, but there I was. Why? Even if the king's messenger came trumpeting up my front step with a stallion and a royal pardon, why would I come to school on a Friday if I didn't have to? Not to see *The Immigrants on Broadway,* that's for sure. I was escaping the child-labor sweatshop at home. Dick had me raking in the mornings, and Mom had me do more mending in the afternoons, now that she knows how good I am. The rest of the time I was writing. Some vacation.

I did notice one change in the building. The sphinx was

gone. So was the Egyptian pyramid mural behind it. I guess Luz was serious about taking it down. They had started to put up the backdrop for another Artist of the Month, but so far there was nothing more than purple paper.

The play was supposed to begin at two o'clock Friday—the last hour of the last day of the week. I wasn't eager to see anyone, so I slipped in at 2:10 when the halls were empty, the whole school was busy admiring Luz, and I was reasonably sure her flute solo would be over.

From the looks of things, I'd been the talk of the school guard community. I sure got plenty of glares from the ones I saw. But I made it into the auditorium, thanks to the note you gave me. I wanted to sit in Row LL. The Loser's Lounge. The Last of the Last. But those seats were all filled. Now that I'm Triple-Parole Tod, I figured I should find an empty seat rather than encourage someone to give me his.

In the darkened auditorium, it was impossible to spot tiny Bernie. He wasn't in the back. But he should have been there somewhere, now that he's back in school. He told me how he spilled his guts to you guys on the Disciplinary Committee. He said he signed a statement about how Rex and Rob beat him up and took his lighter. Bernie surprised me when he said the droogs had been threatening him for being loyal to me. For not selling me out. That's why he was afraid to come to school lately—it wasn't so much about his mom. She's actually doing better.

She was, but I wasn't. I ended up sitting way too close to the stage, a seat from the aisle. Turns out I was right next to

Stuart. He recognized my smell or something, and he said, “Hey, Tod,” when I sat down. Anyway, I won’t give Luz the credit for the packed theater. Why should I? They made everybody come.

And if you think I’m going to write about that play, forget it. On the one hand, it was unbearably stupid. On the other hand, one crazy girl wrote the play, directed the play, got the set built, put up the posters, played the flute, and hoodwinked some random thug into making the costumes.

But man, those were some superior costumes. Here’s my review.

The Boys:

— The Policeman’s buttons didn’t fall off. But his mustache did.
— The Criminal’s shoulders fit his coat.
— The Dad seemed to be taking decent care of Dick’s vest. He ended up wearing it.
— The Landlord’s watch fell off its chain and rolled across the floor. That got one of the only laughs in the play.

The Girls:

— Karen was wearing my dress. Huh?
— The Mother kept pulling at her apron—I thought it would rip.
— The Teacher’s dress had changed. It was the same dress, but different.

There was no reason to pay attention to anything the actors said. I'd already heard too much when I was hiding backstage at the rehearsals. Instead, I marveled at the extra effort Luz took with the teacher's dress. The white circles were now flowers. Dozens of flowers. That was the dress the whole school had seen me modeling on the Internet. Did Luz paint the flowers to protect me, or to separate herself from me? And wouldn't it have been easier just to get another dress? I'll probably never know for sure.

Back to Karen for a moment. I guess she hadn't had her meeting with you and the Disciplinary Committee yet. I remember you said you'd first need to talk to Ricardo, Rashawn, Eric, Jeremy Gibson, and anyone else who might speak up. They wouldn't suspect I'm the source because they've all been afraid to tell me anything. No, good old Karen ended her empire all by herself. So why was she in the dress I made? Maybe Mommy turned down her special shopping request. Doesn't matter. The best part was she looked miserable up there.

And the fake canvas store was back in place. It seemed fine.

How bad was the play? It was so bad, Stuart let me stop describing the so-called action.

At long last (extremely long last), the play ended. Now here's the part that gets me. I know for a fact that 90 percent of the audience was bored out of their brains. So how come they were all standing, hollering, cheering, waving, and acting like the president's motorcade was going by? Because the play was good? No. Because the weekend had begun.

The actors took their bows and stepped back along the set.

The audience began to stand up and leave when Principal CornHoggy appeared out of nowhere and hopped up the stairs. He picked up a microphone, sounding like a bad game-show host who doesn't know he's bad.

"Ladies and gentlemen. Boys and girls. Please be seated. There's just one more thing."

I think *one more thing* is the official hollow promise of our school.

"This performance today is a testimony to what you can do if you want to do it." Then he put his arm out to the audience like an evangelist. "Can you do it?"

I'm pretty sure he wanted us to scream, all together, *Yes we can!* Apparently he's new here. Our school spirit stops at the metal detectors.

Unwilling to admit defeat, Mr. Carnegie next called Luz to the center of the stage. She came out slowly. It was clear the principal was using her as the lone example of actual talent at school. He complimented Luz on the writing, the directing, the production, the posters, the music, the sets, and the costumes.

Through most of this, Luz picked at her fingernails, looking like she wanted to die. But at the mention of the costumes, Luz stepped over and put her hand on the microphone. There was a brutal shriek of feedback—Luz wears large amounts of metal in her ears and around her neck, and I don't think the microphone liked it. Most of us covered our ears.

Luz spoke hesitantly. "Um," she said, "I didn't do the costumes."

This seemed to make no difference to Carnegie, who pulled his microphone back. "Well, then, you bought excellent . . ."

"No," interrupted Luz, leaning into the microphone again but covering her earrings. "The costumes were custom made for the play. I'm just saying I didn't make them."

Sensing that Luz was leading to something, Carnegie tried another approach. "Was it one of your friends, then?"

"Kind of."

This was getting tiring for everyone. Most specifically, me. I was squirming. For no apparent reason, Carnegie was playing a very public game of Hunt Down the Costumer.

"Is your tailor here today?"

Luz put a hand over her eyes to block out the lights. She saw me in the fourth row, made eye contact, but continued to move her hands and eyes across the auditorium for another five seconds. Subtle. Then she leaned into the microphone.

"Yes."

Carnegie seemed totally frustrated. His teachable moment—*You, too, can overachieve in the arts!*—was being railroaded by an invisible costumer. He decided to move beyond Luz and beg the audience directly to end this misery.

"Will the person responsible for the costumes *please* stand up? Then we can all go home and enjoy our weekend!"

Now it was getting interesting. Kids turned their heads and bodies every which way. A murmur came up. Most of these kids don't even know which end of a needle to use. I just slunk down lower in my chair.

For about fifteen months.

And the moment wouldn't end. No matter how much I tried to kill it. It just kept going.

First my fingers moved. Then my arms. Then my legs. Elbows and knees did their jobs. And for reasons I cannot explain, I found myself standing up in front of everyone. It was horrible.

I didn't look up at anyone. I stuffed my hands in my pockets. I stared at my feet. I slouched. The kids directly behind me whispered loudly, "Sit down, man!"

Mrs. Cornell, the head of the English Department, was sitting near me. She leaned over and hissed, "Mr. Munn, *do sit down.*" More voices began to mutter "Munn" and "Munnster" and "Mrs. Munn." Clever stuff like that.

Someone far away yelled, "He did the dresses," and the whole place burst into laughter. I mean everyone. Best laugh of the day. I went red, but I didn't move.

With his assembly in tatters and me in the middle of the mess, Mr. Carnegie was up there seething. "Sentry, please remove that boy."

One of the sentries came down the aisle toward me. He leaned across Stuart and took me by the arm, just above the elbow. I stood unmoving, my eyes down, my hands deeper in my pockets, deeply embarrassed. But also feeling a glimmer of pride. Defiant pride.

The sentry's grip was very tight. I was being dragged toward the aisle and losing my balance. I didn't want to move. I didn't want to fall on Stu, either.

Another blast of feedback filled the auditorium. The sentry loosened his grip out of pain, I'm sure. Luz had taken the microphone straight from Carnegie's hand.

"He did the costumes. It's true. Tod sewed them himself. That's why he was getting dresses and stuff. He was making the costumes."

Suddenly there wasn't any noise in the room except the tail end of the electronic feedback. Sometimes they say the silence echoes. This was definitely one of those times.

Everyone's eyes were on me. Me. Tod Munn. And I have to admit it. I didn't mind.

But, true to character, I slipped into the aisle and past the sentry, who had already let go. I walked up the aisle to the doors. And I turned around. Not to face the staring crowd, but to push the door's bar open with my butt. Like always.

Like Tod Munn.

Wednesday, December 8

One more thing, Mrs. Woodrow. Then I'm done.

On that night you came to my house and read my notebook, we talked about nicknames and busting classmates and so on. Then you got up and looked around my house, pretending to stretch your neck but actually seeing what the word *underprivileged* really means.

"Now if you'll excuse me, Tod, I should be going."

But I didn't move off your coat.

"Can I ask you a question, Mrs. W.?"

"You *may* ask me any question, Tod."

After hesitating a few seconds to gather my words, I knew what I wanted to say.

"You've definitely gone above and beyond. I mean, with your attempts to reform a loser like me. So, why?"

I think you were playing coy, because you smiled.

"Why? Why what, Tod?"

"Why all this? Why me? You didn't expel me when we broke into the school. Or when I busted Ricardo's glasses. You spent a ton of time watching me scribble gibberish every afternoon instead of making me pick garbage off the baseball diamond. And now you're here in my lovely home, trying to save my neck again. So? Why?"

Now it was your turn to stop and think.

And, finally, you said, "Tod, I've been looking at your case for two years. Yes, your grades are excellent. But, by any other measure, you should have been cut out of our school community long ago. You should have been tossed into the juvie with the rest of the career criminals. The morning you were hauled up in front of the Disciplinary Committee after breaking into the school and vandalizing our property, I was ready to expel the lot of you. If I'd had a gavel I would have pounded it on your head. When I stood at my podium and asked you what your excuse was, your friends were silent. But *you* didn't back down. Do you remember what you told me?"

"You mean about the sign?"

"Absolutely."

"I looked you straight in the eye, and I reminded you what's on every school door:

NO TRESPASSING VIOLATORS

WILL BE PROSECUTED

And since we were trespassing violators . . . the sign said we wouldn't be prosecuted."

You nodded. I broke into a huge grin.

"Was *that* all that kept us from getting kicked out of school?"

And you smiled back at me.

"Yes."

Acknowledgments

Now that I've learned what it takes to write a novel, I understand why writers set aside a page full of gratitude for those who generously handed out water and encouragement along the marathon route.

First and most importantly, I am indebted to Neal Porter, my editor and friend. Neal suggested I write this book, and he used subtle, wise, and devious techniques to help make sure I finished it. Without Neal's immeasurable involvement, this book simply would not exist.

Harold Underdown and Emily Herman gave me advice and insights into the writing process that I will never forget. And when I had wandered into the maze, the wonderful and patient Caroline Chinlund helped me find a way out.

Thank you to my volunteer corps of first readers: Kara the magnificent, who responded to every single chapter, as well as Esther, Barbara, Ellie, Leah, and Miriam. And thanks to the friends who were kind enough to lend an ear, give support, and drop some hints: Nancy Werlin, Alison James, Cleve Lamison, Amy Krouse Rosenthal, Eric Luper, and Leslie Ann Kent. Then there's the high school teacher I'll always remember—the one who inspired me to write. His name is Ken Wilson.

And finally, to you, the reader, who read this page: I hope you liked it. The book, I mean. All these people helped me when I asked for help. But you're the person I wrote it for.

—Mark Shulman

QUESTIONS FOR MARK SHULMAN ABOUT SCRAWL

Mark Shulman had a lot of different jobs before he began writing books. However, all of them had to do with making stuff up. Now, Mark has the strangest job yet—to answer questions about his own book.

What's your short summary of *Scrawl*?
Scrawl is the story of Tod Munn, a tough kid from a bad neighborhood. And he's in big trouble. The book is a journal he's been forced to write as a condition of his not going to juvie.

Everyone thinks they've figured Tod out: He's supposed to be a bully and a thug, and a budding criminal—and he likes that they've got it wrong. Every day after school, he's stuck with a guidance counselor who sees something in Tod that is actually right. He's smart and clever, and funny, all liabilities in Tod's world.

As Tod goes through the short time period of the book, he's forced to reckon with his gang of friends, setting a path for himself that will either lead to bigger trouble or redemption. It sounds grim, but it's actually quite funny.

Do you remember writing the first words of the story? Are they still the same?
Not only are they the same, but I figured out how to put them in the front of the book. You meet Tod at the point I met Tod—during a random writing exercise. I was just writing about glasses, and suddenly, I was this big kid busting another kid's glasses in my old high school. But Tod's detached, like an art expert, while he considers the finer points of beating a kid up. He was so fascinating, I wrote a book around him.

What kind of research did you have to do for this story?
I closed my eyes and thought about the layout of my old high school. Since I spent six highly formative years there, it was easy to set the stage. Having a fundamental blueprint of the school made all the difference in what's where and how to get there. One other tool was Google Calendar. Since the book is told entirely in journal form, the

days and dates had to click. The book is set on the same calendar as 2010.

Did you say high school took six years?
It was a junior/senior high school. Grades 7–12. But yeah, some of the students were 19, 20. I arrived as a little pink 12-year-old. Imagine, for a moment, the gym classes.

What is the hardest part of writing for you?
For me, writing is like one of those huge science-museum soap bubbles you create with a large hoop. A number of circumstances need to be in place: the environment, the lack of interference, and a steady focus on my part. Of course, when I'm crushing under deadline, all I need is some coffee and another hour.

What one question do you wish an interviewer would ask you, but never has?
"Is the female lead, Luz, based on a real person?"

None of my characters are real people. Some are composite and some are entirely fictional. Luz, the artsy goth girl, is a favorite of mine because she muscled her way into the book far more than I expected. She was supposed to have a bit part, but she and Tod started talking, and there were sparks. Not romantic sparks. More like the pre-romantic way two teenagers might use each other as knife-sharpening wheels. In their particular public school, there isn't so much high-intellectual wattage. So despite themselves, they're drawn together. That's how she promoted herself from a supporting role in one scene to a lead role in several.

Hey, I didn't answer my own question. Luz is a composite of a few girls I knew in school. But she's also quite a work of fiction.

How did you become a writer?
I got an old Royal manual typewriter for my eleventh or twelfth birthday. I've always liked rearranging people and events into my own stories, and I've been at it ever since. In high school, I wrote comics and a sci-fi magazine, and parodies of the school paper I would publish and sell. I've written advertising, tours, bad TV scripts, worse stand-up comedy, positioning papers, more advertising, CEO

speeches, radio contests, a very funny menu for a hot dog restaurant in New York City's garment district, cover letters, corporate videos, poems, apologies to traffic court judges, and anything even remotely resembling advertising. Then, I met a wonderful teacher, married her, and started to write books for kids. All kinds of books: nonfiction, picture books, preschool, novelty, movie tie-ins, TV tie-ins, books that contain glowing monster heads, voodoo dolls, trivia quizzes, and humor, celebrity picture books, quote books, books with snails that slide around the page, and a novel.

What is your favorite line, passage, chapter from this book?
"I like reading. It's free travel."

Was there any part that you struggled with or avoided writing?
Oh, yes. There's a point about one third of the way when Tod is going to make a defining choice. It's one of those early winter afternoons when the weather is bleak and the sky is prematurely dark and he does NOT want to be in this place making this choice to be a good guy or bad guy. So, he's standing outside a door and he freezes up. So did I. Got to admit, I hated the moment as much as he did. Then the phone rang, and I was offered some nonfiction book projects. I took them all. Many moons later, I picked up this book again, having received a piece of invaluable advice: Write the part after this scene, and then come back to it. How simple! And how very, very effective.

Besides writing, do you have any other passions?
New York City, jazz, architecture, history, going on drives. And my family. We're a tight group.

What are your hobbies?
New York City, jazz, architecture, history, going on drives. And my family. Also, every two years, I follow politics the way other guys follow sports.

Have you ever wanted to quit writing? Why?
Yes. Because it's hard. And then I remember that all work is hard,

and lots of it is harder than writing. But not as much fun, so I don't quit.

What is one piece of advice you'd want to give a starting writer?

Two pieces. The first is: Don't quit. You already are a writer. You see things, you think about them, you have an opinion, you tell a story. That's writing. Just put it down on paper. Then other people can share your ideas. Don't stop, and you'll see how the hand-to-paper part gets easier and easier.

My second piece of advice is to learn to type. Really learn it. And type well—35, 40, 50 words a minute. You like video games? Get typing software, it's full of games and nobody will tell you to stop playing. Imagine how good it will be when your ideas just magically appear upon the computer. No effort, just flowing from your brain to your fingers. School papers, e-mails, and jobs will be far easier. Forever.

If you could be anything else besides a writer, what would it be?

I'd like to design things. My mind is always at work improving backpacks, carts, kitchen setups, lamps, toys, car accessories, and room layouts. I'm especially keen on inventing clever, multipurpose objects that nobody's ever seen before. I don't think there's a career in that, though.

Tell us something about you that no one knows.

I've got O-type blood, which makes me the universal pincushion. What's more, my blood hasn't got antigens, so even fragile people won't reject it. That makes me extremely desirable, hematologically. So, I give blood as often as I can. We folks have to stick together. So, go out there and give it up.

This interview was originally conducted by YA author Melissa Wyatt for her excellent blog. Used with permission.

QUESTIONS FOR YOU ABOUT *SCRAWL*

As the narrator, Tod has complete control over what the reader learns. But he still reveals things he didn't intend to. What's something about Tod you think he tried to hide? Why would he want to hide it?

Each member of Tod's "gang"—Rex, Rob, and Bernie—brings out a different side of his personality. So does Luz. Use examples to describe each of these relationships. What is Tod like when he's with each person? What is he like when he's with the whole gang?

Would you call Tod a "real" bully? Why or why not?

What are some of the ways that Tod's writing assignment helps him see himself and his world differently?

Over the story, the relationship between Tod and Mr. Harmon changes. Where did they start, where did they end up, and why?

What is the importance of the sphinx statue in the story?

Based on what you know, what could Tod, Rex, Rob, and Bernie be like as adults? Is there evidence that any of them might change paths?

Tod and Luz each have many natural talents. What's different about how they use those talents? What are some similarities they share?

Twice in the story, Tod faces being expelled. Imagine you are Mrs. Woodrow talking to the principal. What would you say to persuade him not to expel Tod at the beginning of the book, and again, at the end?

Over the course of the book, does Tod's relationship with his mother and Dick change? What makes you think so?

What is the reason Tod gives for agreeing to help Luz? What might be another, deeper reason?

Tod says, "I like reading. It's free travel." What does this sentence mean to Tod? What does it mean to you?

Bullying isn't all hitting and stealing. Name some of the different kinds of bullying that goes on in *Scrawl*.

Knowing what you know about Tod, what would you say to him if he asked you for money in school?

Knowing what you know about Greg or Karen, what would you say if they asked you to join their group?